The Chronicles Of Riley and Bella

The Beginning Of Magic

To all the animals of the world. Especially
dogs and horses.
S.T
To anyone who feels lost in the world.
S.E.

The Beginning of Magic

By Shrutee Takale & Sabine Erbrecht

CONTENTS

Introduct Tape. No. Introduction   7

Chapter One   9

Chapter Two   34

Chapter Three   64

Chapter Four   78

Chapter Five   92

Chapter Six   102

Chapter Seven   120

Chapter Eight   125

Chapter Nine   134

Chapter Ten   139

Chapter Eleven   142

Chapter Twelve   146

Chapter Thirteen   155

Chapter Fourteen   157

Chapter Fifteen   171

Chapter Sixteen   183

Chapter Seventeen   196

ABOUT THE AUTHORS   215

Acknowledgements   217

Introduct Tape. no. Introduction

The bloodthirsty vampires moved toward my helpless parents. I watched in awe and horror. How did vampires even exist? How did they get here? Why are they even here? Were they coming for revenge? For the fun of it? All I knew was that *this* wasn't *'fun.'* My parents and I were walking—I was riding Buddy, my horse— along a stone path in the countryside—Our part of Texas is just countryside DUH—and all of a sudden a colony of small, yet *purple* bats came swooping down and magically turned into vampires!

The roaring thunder crashed to the spine-chilling notes of horror. My horse and I galloped away from danger. His nimble hooves clomped quickly on the hard, slippery path. <Boom!>

"Riley! Save yourself!" screamed my mother, as a ghostly hand started closing around her neck. She looked strangely calm though.

7

Weird.

"MOM!" I screamed, wanting to scoop her up, but no matter how many times I stepped in, I had to back away. "DAD!"

I wanted to go back there. I wanted to take Mom and Dad with me. I wanted them to be *safe*.

"Zut up, voman, iv you vant doo live!" scolded a mysterious, ghastly man, shaking his bony finger. I rode away into the dark shadows without a reply.

I looked at my parents for the last time, though I didn't know it yet.

<Boom!>

My father remained silent. The vampires snarled and sneered as they closed on him. I took a deep breath. I would have to leave my parents behind. I know they would want me to. I steered around the tall evergreen trees. One of the trees came in the way and I almost rammed into it! Then, one of the horrible vampires wheeled around and sped-flew toward me! She was six feet tall, wearing no cape, black slippers, and a long, black, Victorian dress. She had long black hair, which seemed to get in her eyes.

<Clap-a-boom!>

"How can she fly so fast in a dress? And how can she see with all the hair?!" I wondered, looking back.

As the woman caught up, I disappeared into a clump of wet, green needles. I hid behind my panting horse until the eerie vampires were gone.

"Oh. My. Gosh. How did I even SURVIVE that? Are my mom and dad dead?!" The answer, unfortunately, was...

...yes.

Yes, my poor parents died that tragic night. The fatal vampires were my new powerful enemies. Sworn. For. Life.

It couldn't be true! But it was!

Vampires were real! That was official. Well, for me, anyway. I guess I would be one of the only people to know about them. Why me?

I still have terrible nightmares about the mournful event. I always have. But, I didn't realize the *magic* that was about to come. My life would change.

Forever.

Chapter One

My perfect Life, until *some* vampires ruined it
Five Days Ago

"Dad. We. *Must.* Have. A. Horse." I begged my dad, who was sitting in a chair, for the one hundred billionth time. I think I was starting to turn into a snob. Wah. But that was five days ago! Who cares?

"Please, Riley. You are thirteen years old. You mustn't whine anymore." Mom came into the room.

"Riley, how about when you're seventeen?" she asked, raising her eyebrows. She wore a silk white blouse, with long, blue jeans on the bottom. Her tanned face had a stern expression.

"WHY DO I HAVE TO WAIT FOR *FOUR* YEARS!?!" I groaned.

Our maid, Anna, waltzed into the room too. Her top teeth poked out of her mouth.

Talk about manners. My mom says never to let your teeth show when your mouth is closed.

Mom is a famous model, a veterinarian, and a businesswoman.

She has a lotta lotta lotta money.

Anna took out a notepad and took the pen from her ear.

"Would you like a peanut butter and jelly sandwich?" she asked.

"I won't eat a single micrograin of food until you get me a horse. Period," I protested, rudely. I knew I was rude, but it was TOTALLY worth it.

Totally.

Anna looked stricken, as if someone hit her with something. Drama queen.

My parents have a soft spot for Anna.

"Riley! Apologize to Anna this INSTANT!" scowled Mom, wagging her finger in my face.

"Sorry," I grumbled very loudly, so Anna, my parents, and I could hear. "Sorry you are so dramatic and sorry you ask for the wrong food!" I also added. "I like crepes. Or other food. Not snails. Ew."

Big mistake.

11

"Riley! You're grounded!" Mom fumed so much, I could see cartoon smoke coming from her ears. Humph.

I was forced to my room and I almost got into a fit, but I cooled it.

After all, I *am* a young adult. Naw, a teenager is more like it.

A few boring, long hours later, (I wasn't grounded anymore), I peered over the huge-grand-white oak staircase as I heard my parents whisper 'Riley' 'horse' and 'get one for her.'

"Yes!" My parents were finally going to get a horse for me!

My mom started up the stairs. I quickly—and quietly— tip-toed into my bedroom so that they wouldn't know that I'd been eavesdropping on their 'important' Riley's horse conversation. I pretended to read a book. Doopity Doopity Doo. I'm reading a book. *Not eavesdropping on my parents.* "Riley, we have a very *epicawesomeverycoolyoucan'twaitforit* news!" said my mom, grinning as she entered my room. She has a VERY weird way of telling good news. Why? When I was little, I

12

liked it. When I was VERY LITTLE. My mom once even forgot my age!

When I was turning TEN, she thought I was turning *eight*. She is very busy, and I barely get to see her. Today she just came back from Paris. The housekeeper, Betty, looks after me. Alia, my babysitter doesn't, because she went back to college for a pharmacy and doctor PhD. She's now a doctor at our local hospital. "You are old enough for a horse." Mom said.

● ● ●

When we got to the horse stables the next day, there were five horses for sale! A blood bay horse, a dapple gray, an Irish Cob/Gypsy Pony, a Missouri Fox Trotter, and a blinding white stallion. The stallion was athletic, masculine. Very gracious, gentle. I chose the beautifully delicate and calm stallion. His mane was gleaming like shiny pearls. I stroked his silky, soft coat.
"He's friendly," I said happily. I was relieved that none of them bit me, or bucked at me.

"You don't actually want to sell all these horses, do you?" I asked, out of curiosity. A man gasped. "YOU ARE THE PETERSONS!!!!!" He shouted. Lots of people started charging towards us, phones ready to snap selfies. After the selfie stampede left, the man who was showing the horses cleared his throat, looking very 'official'.

"They all are friendly." The man with the Scottish accent said, showing them off. His lines looked practiced. I imagined an hour before the sale, he was standing in front of his bathroom mirror, like, *"Suppose a person says, 'Hey! These horses are cool!' What would I say? How about, 'They are cool!' Naw, how about* 'They are aaaaaall friendly!!!!' *Yessiree. This is goody,"* while adjusting his plaid bow tie.

One of the horses, a blood bay (COLOR), one with a blaze marking on his face, neighed as if to say, *"Yeah! You are right! We are nice.*

"<Neigh> Wrong of that rude farmer to get rid of us five. <Neigh.> He kicked me square in the delicate hindquarters, so I kicked him in the face. <Neigh>.

"Hehhey, that was <neigh> funny. He still has that hoof scar. <Neigh> Hey! If I ever do come back here, <neigh> I'll show him what more I can do. There's a lot I could do to that wretched farmer......<NEIGH!> Ha! I guess I should shut up now before that ghastly farmer dude starts getting ticked off again. <Neigh!> Hahaha!!!! <NEIGH!!!!>"

14

He had a southern wavering accent that trembled like the notes on my viola when I played on the bow and it squeaked and squawked like a wounded pig.

I didn't know how I understood, but THAT horse? He TALKED.

Never mind. The Texas heat must have played tricks to my head.

"What are you gonna name him?" Mom asked. His name actually was Buddy, because it was on the halter. "Buddy," I said. "His name's Buddy. I love him."

Glancing at the huge crowd starting to gather, I took off. Mom and Dad were busy paying for Buddy.

I went to the gift shop. Seriously! A gift shop on a farm! The doorbell rang. *Ding Ding!* There were people everywhere!

"How may I help you? OMG! You are Riley Peterson!!" Gasped the store clerk, excitedly. She was a teenage girl with light brown hair tied in green pigtails with a green plaid ribbon and green suspenders. Green boots. I think I know her favorite color and her favorite habit, 'cause I see a picture frame with the girl. Wearing a green dress, green socks, green shoes, and green *I'mgonnathrowup* face.

I guess she was going to dress up as a lawn for Halloween. Or a green vegetable.

Ick.

Never eat green dairy. Chances are it might be moldy. Minus the vegetables. They turn white and fuzzy when moldy. Not a good sign. Unless it is celery, I dunno about that. So NEVER eat green cheese. Only blue cheese from the market. Make sure THAT isn't past the expiration date. I didn't once, and *boy,* did I have the *worst* stomach aches.

Anyway, the girl's name must've been Jessica since it said it on her name tag. She looked like she was seventeen.

I said, "Yes, and I'm looking for horse supplies. Can you please tell me where they are?"

"Oh, they are just there, over by the chicken feed!" said the girl.

She pointed to the shelf where all the chicken and horse stuff are. "I STILL CAN'T BELIEVE RILEY PETERSON IS HERE!!!!!!!!" Jessica shrieked. Typical.

"WHAT!?!?!?" The other people shrieked too when they saw me.

15 minutes later, my hand ached from all the handshakes and my face hurt from smiling so hard in selfies. Ugh.

16

Another customer called Jessica over to help find something and she went to see it with her customer.

I, on the other hand, went over to the massive shelf with horse supplies.

I bought horse food and tack. A purple halter, a lead rope, a Western saddle, a bridle, a brush, a hoof pick, and a lot of other horse stuff. Plus a small horse magazine. Five dollars.

The whole amount was two hundred fifty something bucks or something.

I paid for the stuff from the money in my allowance. I've saved for this stuff for 3 whole years! I didn't spend a single cent from my allowance for two years! Even if it is super duper tempting and my hand itched to get that awesome blue T-shirt with Pegasus on it or that skateboard I had been dying to get.

Actually, as I looked closer, I got that skateboard for my birthday anyway. Not the shirt.

I could have imagined that I came to school in that Pegasus shirt while doing an ollie and a Laser Flip. Everyone would be oohing and ahhing at my grand entrance. The wind would be blowing on my hair....

When I came to school with my skateboard, it rained so my hair was wet and clung to my head; when I tried doing just a little trick, I fell and landed on my butt. I had abandoned my skateboard after that. That felt like it happened just yesterday! Though I don't go to public school anymore.

I exited the gift shop and found my parents. "C'mon. Let me ride Buddy home while you guys use the car," I said.

My parents exchanged a worried glance.

"Honey, are you sure that you can keep up with the car, not get trampled by other cars *and* not get lost? We're going on a highway," Mom asked.

"Of course, I can! It saves energy! You guys go ahead and I'll follow after I tack up Buddy. By the way, I know a shortcut home that has NO highways," I reassured my parents.

"Hey! Who's the grown-up?" My dad asked, a teasing tone in his voice.

"Me!" I shot back, grinning. Almost.

The next day, I tacked up Buddy and went for a ride. I thought that people would give me quizzical looks, but they didn't since horses are common here, in the country. *Silly me*! The countryside in Texas is the best place for mansions 'cause where we live, literally everyone lives in mansions. We live in the Great Plains in an uncharted place. It's *not* Austin. My mom just says that so that the paparazzi won't be chasing us. Mom's a very famous model, *of course*, and Dad's a millionaire. Of course we'd be in the *news*. *I* was. I was a TV commercial model and in the front page of some magazines before I moved here. I hated it, though. People shouldn't judge other girls based on their *looks*. It's their personality that counts. Anyway, I don't want people to look around saying, "EEK! IT'S RILEY PETERSON!!! CAN I GET A SELFIE?!!?!?!?!?!?!?!?"

I want to be *free*.

Buddy's hooves made a funny clacking clomping sound. We moved in a rhythm. *Clop-clop-clop-clop clop-clop*. I felt one with Buddy as I moved him into a canter. *Gallop-clop   clop-gallop-gallop-clop-clop-clop-clop-clop-gallop-gallop-gallop-trot-tr ot-gallop*.

It felt like my skin melted into his, my arms felt like they melted into his, my legs, my midsection, everything, making us one, hideous looking (trust me, a human and a horse mixed *would* look VERY monstrous) animal.

But maybe not with me, because I am a Sagittarius.

I moved him into a full gallop.

The world was a blur as we zoomed through the miles of open space, still open, ahead of us. It felt like flying! Literally! When Buddy made a happy leap, he soared so high, I thought he was going to FLY INTO THE SKY.

"Wooooooooo-*hooooooo*!!!"

It's the most awesome feeling in the world! The world was our oyster! The birds chirped happily in the summer morning to make things even better! I will never forget this feeling ever in my life!

Even when I'm, like, 90 and am an old lady and have dementia.

We went back home. I gave Buddy a little drink, and I evened out the sweat on his back. My white sneakers squished under the dewey grass. I took off my shoes, yelled "I'M HOME, MOM!!!!!!!!!!!" (even though Mom tells me not to ever yell in our mansion. I did it on purpose.) and went into my room and wrote in my diary about our thrilling ride.

"Dear Diary,

Today, my new horse and I went for an amazing ride. We were so fast!

My horse, Buddy, was sooo good! He's like the most perfect horse....."

I wrote a lot in my fuzzy blue diary. It had a gold print saying 'My name is Riley, Animal Lover' in swirly cursive.

My special sponsors/maids made it. On every page, a dog's, horse's or hedgehog's face is on the side. I only wrote and drew about my dog in it, or my experiences and interactions with other animals.

I sighed about my wonderful life.

Mom came into my room without knocking or asking permission.

<GASP!!!!> MY LIFE IS HORRIBLE!!!!!!!!!!

Nah, I'm just kidding. I'm not a *snobby* rich girl.

"Hi, my honey bunny. Whatcha doing? Ohh...your diary. I think the dog looks like General Puppy." Mom says.

There are also dog pictures on forty-eight percent of the diary.

"Mom, it's not only General Puppy. Also, stop reading my private entries!" I ordered.

General Puppy, my dog came into my room and his ears perked up curiously at mentioning his name. I ruffled his cute floppy ears. His tongue lolled out and he padded out of my powder blue and rose quartz pink spacious room.

My mom said, "Riley, how's your horse? And anyways, do you like living in the country? Are you homesick? Do you miss the city?"

"Naw, not a bit! I love it here," I said, reassuringly.

Mom gave me *the look.*

Huh.

Something's fishy. Four years ago, I used to live in the city, in Boston, but then we moved here, in Texas, for my health or something. I vomited, blacked out, and had intense, wait for it, wait for it, DIARRHEA!!! Okay. Throw up all you want. Laugh at me. I don't care. Anyway, I just love it here! But it is quite odd for Mom to ask something like that.

I don't know why I was sick. I felt nauseated all the time and the world started spinning when I stood up. Mom sorta knew what was wrong with me. I was 9 at the time, and she used to say, *"Riley, you'll see the future now,"* while stroking my sweaty hair. And when I started to accidentally burn stuff up when we moved here, (I was fine now) she said, *"Oh Riley, the future of Olympus lies in your hands. Use your fire properly."* She said this all when Dad wasn't there and she insisted us to play Olympus Magic. Or something.

Or something.

Oh well. Who cares! I wrote some more in my fuzzy blue diary.

Then I doodled in my gigantic drawing notebook. Five hundred pages. Fifty percent are already occupied.

YE YE YE-AH! Stop. Brain. I order you to STOP.

YE YE YE-AH!! STOOOOOOOOOOOOP! BRAIN! STOOOOOOOOOOOOOOOOOOOOOOOOOOOOOOOP! I RULE YOU!!!! SO I ORDER YOU TO STOP THAT STUPID FREAKIN SONG!!!

Okay.

Song stopped.

Ye ye ye-ah!

Ugh.

I drew a picture of General Puppy. His bubblegum pink long tongue hangs out of his drooling mouth. His amber eyes seem so real. I took an art class two months ago. His floppy brown ears prick as he sees a cat. I drew the cat's long tail. General Puppy chases the poor, terrified cat. The scene is the huge park.

I doodled another picture.

This time, I drew a horse. He was pitch black. Like a Friesian horse. Black like midnight with blonde spots on his dark snout. 'Starry Night' I named him. I put a label on my smooth paper. I tried to write neatly, but it was a little hard for me. My hands were shaky. It came out like this:

STARRY NIGHT, not *Starry Night*, like how I usually write.

Huh. This is how I wrote back in Boston!

All shaky and messy. Weird.

'I don't know why....but maybe it's something important and I don't know it. Or maybe it's just something's wrong with my body again...... or maybe it's something I forgot. Who cares,' I thought.

But probably since I needed to move to Texas for my health, (or something) *that's* why my hands are shaky!

No, no, it couldn't be.

But maybe...

No! Riley, pace yourself. You're an over-thinker! Just calm down and draw some more.

See? Never mind. I forgot about my shaking hands.

Augh! Stupid, stupid!

I got tired a few doodled horse drawings later and went to the massive dining room since I was as hungry as a bear. I politely told Chef Dana to make me grilled cheese sandwiches. *Two* appetizing, luscious, creamy, cheese-filled grilled cheese sandwiches. In fifteen minutes, (I was more famished than ever!!!) a plate of two heaping grilled cheese sandwiches were in front of me. I quickly devoured the absolutely scrumptious sandwiches. The taste of melty, smoky cheddar cheese and fontina val d'aosta (cheddar for one, fontina for the other.) with the familiar crunchy french toast filled my mouth. "Mmmm....." I said to Chef Dana.

"Thanks, Riley. I like it when I get complimented," she said, looking over her glasses.

"Hey what's that over there?" I asked, pointing, my mouth still sorta filled with those heavenly, mouthwatering sandwiches!

A flashlight was shining.
Chef Dana squinted as she rubbed her foggy, clouded spectacles.

"Oh! That's the search party, looking for that lost dog!" I exclaim, remembering that a few days ago, there was a LOST DOG notice in the newspaper.

"I don't think so...," she trailed off.

"Never mind." I shrugged and excused myself from the table.

I watched a movie on my TV. It's cool. It's about horses and they are wild horses, and humans are trying to tame them for some reason. Seriously, guys? They're WILD HORSES!!! They're called 'wild' for a reason, you know. But they are ponies, really. Then humans come and capture them. The horses finally get relocated to an uncharted island.

The next morning, I went to play soccer with my best friend, Bella. "Hey! Goal!!" Bella whooped. Her long, twisty copper strawberry-colored hair curls bounced up and down in a ponytail as the sun highlighted it into a light golden color. "This is great practice. You're so good at it—like me!" Bel laughed. Her white striped soccer uniform had Hamilton, 10 on the back. Mine was white striped and had Peterson, 7. Lucky Ducky me. The rest of the girls from our soccer team were taking a break, but not us!

"You aren't *twice* as good as me!" I bragged, lovingly. Bella knew it was just a joke. She always says stuff like that to me, but she's not all snooty or stuck-up. Not in a taunting way, at least.

Her small phone dinged, and she read her new text, and typed back. She flipped the top of her phone down.

"'Kay, I gotta go home right now, you can come with me and stay for dinner, if you want," she offered.

"I'd love to," I said. I would never miss an opportunity to go to the Hamiton's (Bella's) house. It is so fancy, and Bella's sister, Stephanie, has an awesome taste in music! As I caught up with her, I found Buddy galloping across a field in my horse paddock my parents immediately built.

"Oh, and Bella! Meet Buddy, my new horse!" I said, showing Buddy off to her.

"Oh, he's so adorable!" she said, walking over to him.

"Isn't he beautiful?" I asked. Bella nodded in amazement.

"Would you like to pet him?"

"Would I—?!--- YES!!" She walked over to him, held out her palm and Buddy sniffed it. I think he must have been saying in his head (if horses could talk), *Ooh! New girl! Mmmm... Hand smells like cinnamon and banana scented soap! Sweat! Ick. Nail polish remover? Oooh, better stay away from that. Smells like... red. Ooh ooh! Blueberry muffin crumbs inside of her nails?! NO FAIR! HOW DID SHE GET TO HAVE THAT!?!"*

"I love you!" Bella squealed like a pterodactyl. She did it quietly. She wouldn't want to startle a horse, because, well, let's just say things could end *badly*. "Let's go, though. I don't want to get my mom too mad!"

I nodded my head in agreement.

"Good point." I gave Buddy a big hug and patted his nose. "Now you be a good boy." I giggled. He neighed. I jogged over to Bella and blew him a kiss.

I stopped when we finally got there. I panted. Bella and I just stopped from a race to her house. She's a pretty competitive person, and I'm usually pretty fast, so she loves being friends with me.

Bella and I knocked vigorously on the door, red faced, breathing hard and filling our bellies with unstoppable giggling.

"Good evening, girls!" Bella's mom said.

"Hi, Mom," Bella said.

"Hi, Ms. Hamilton!" I said.

"Come in, Riley. Bella needs to finish her homework. Meanwhile, you can watch TV or play video games," Ms. Hamilton said.

"Actually, can I help you make dinner?" I asked. I always like to help out around their house ever since Bella's mom broke her ankle. "Of course! We're making Denver omelets," she said.

"Come in! You're probably tired after practice." I went close to the door and dusted my shoes off on the welcome mat. "Thanks for coming, Riley."

"Of course," I said.

"I made you some treats. I figured you girls must be hungry after all that running," Mrs. Hamilton said, offering a sfogliatella from a big basket. "Starving. Riley scored a goal, and I kicked the ball farther than the planet Neptune from here! Oooh! Sfogliatella! And cannolis!" Bella exaggerated, grabbing one of the cannoli from the basket. "Hey, Ri, can you help me with my homework?" asked Bella. "Sure," I said, as we ran giggling upstairs.

"...And that's why the square root of 4 is 2." I explained. "Oh, yeah! I totally get that now!" she exclaimed, proudly. The room went silent for a minute except for the scribbling of Bella's pencil.

"It's been so quiet ever since...," she started. She was a quiet mouse. "Mom and dad got divorced."

I rubbed her back.

"Yeah. Oh, I'm so sorry, Bella!" I said, soothing her.

"It's fine," She sighed, forcing a smile, her braced teeth slightly showing. She started breathing quickly and heavily.

"Okay, done." Bella sniffled. I started fussing with her hair until she gave her paper to me.

"Can you check it?" she asked.
"Sure." I looked at her paper.

"Um. I... Don't... Really... Know. Lol. But, I think you got something wrong on number 5." I said, helpfully.

"Okay," She looked carefully at the question and just stared at it. I could tell she was confused, so I whispered into her ear what the problem was.

"Mhm. I think I get it...," she said, and went off scratching her eraser on the homework.

"You are so smart! Did your mom and dad teach you this or something?" Bella asked.

"Yeah, kinda," I replied.

I just heard loud heavy metal music roaring from Stephanie's room.

"Turn it down, Steph!" Bella argued.

Stephanie just ignored her.

"Ste-eph!!"

"Bel-la!" Stephanie teased.

I giggled.

Stephanie found Bella's personality quite boisterous.

"Trust me, Riley! This friend you have right now! Well, you're making a big mistake for a friend. Unless you like rowdy!" Stephanie scoffed.

"Nah. I like Bella the way she is just fine," I disagreed.

Bella nodded her head, happily. "Yeah, Stephanie Mcjerky Poopingpants! You should be grateful," Bella taunted.

Stephanie ignored Bella and just blasted the music louder.

"Riley, Bella, can you help me make dinner?" Called Mrs. Hamilton, loudly.

"Coming!" I told her, racing down the steps.

I dipped an egg into the sizzling pan. It was hissing like a snake.

"Be careful, Riley! Don't get burned!" Mrs. Hamilton said, anxiously.

"I won't," I assured her. "And stop worrying so much! Are you okay?"

"I'm okay. Bel's okay. Stephanie's...not okay. She's not handling the divorce very well. She's been teasing me, Bella, and her father lately." Mrs. Hamilton said, now even more worried than the last time.

"There's no need to be depressed, Ms. Hamilton. She'll get over it. Give her time. At least, that's what my mom says to me," I advised her.

"Thank you," she said.

After dinner, Bella and I played a video game on her Nintendo Switch

"You're on fire!" I yelled.

"Well, thank you," she joked.

"Not in that way," I told her. I was almost at the end when, *Ding!* I heard my phone going off. I got a text from my dad. He asked where I was.

Me: I'm at Bella's house.

Dad: Can U come back?

Me: Ye.

"Okay, Bella, I gotta go." I said, slipping my light pink phone in my pocket.

"Awww, I was so close to beating you!" she whined, smiling at me.

"Bye!" I said.

"Stay awesome! Say hi to Buddy for me!" Bella told me, as I was heading over to my home.

Me: Why do I have 2 come home???? I was playing with Bel ☹

Dad: U have to come home. It's dinner time.

Me: KK ☹

I walked along the path. I almost ran into a tree while walking and texting! I looked up and walked more carefully.

Chapter Two

In the Present

I Get a Really Weird Dream, That's All I'm Gonna Tell You.

I wake up in a bush full of dry prickly pine needles.

"Buddy, boy! Where could you be?" I ask, in a daze. Then, a flash of bad, evil memories from last night burns my brain through, as it all floats slowly back to me. My parents screaming in fear, "Riley! Go!" "Riley! Save yourself!" "Riley!" "Riley!" "Riley..."

I shake my head like a wet dog.

Memories gone. There.

"Buddy!! Come out, come out, wherever you AA-ARE!!" I call. Suddenly, I hear a loud huff from seven feet away. <Whinny!> I hear a sound. I walk over.

I gasp, as I meet the terror in his dark hazel eyes. I face the bloody stuff on his spine and hindquarters. His white coat is smeared with sticky blood. He lets out a breathy nicker. His hazel eyes are starting to go GLASSY! He's gonna die, if he doesn't get better! I remember when a guy at the beach near Boston jumped into shallow water and there was blood all over his head and his skull literally was broken and his scalp had fallen off and we could see his brain, and there was this gooey clear liquid and...he's not with us anymore???

"Oh, boy!" I scream in fear, tears stinging my eyes. "Please! No!" I whisper, loudly.

I have to think of a plan. And fast! There is no vet nearby in the middle of nowhere. I rip up the bottom of my shirt and use it as a bandage, trying to find where the wounds were coming from. *Wow, what a bad cloth.*

I find one, and I wrap the piece of cloth around his body tightly. The wounds look horrible! It looks as if a cougar scratched right through his skin! What if there's a hungry cougar, -cue the tummy grumble- nearby?!

I look around to see if there is anything out of the blue to be seen.

Nothing.

I snap my attention back to my severely wounded horse.

"Do you feel better?" I coo.

I soothingly stroke his forelock. I ask him to stand up.

He does.

How?!

When I sit on him, he doesn't buck or yelp in pain or anything too bad! That's great.

But he isn't much better. Not yet, at least.

Medicine!

I know how to make some out of long, prickly pine needles. I know just what to do, since my mother is-or, *was* a veterinarian.

FYI, my mom was a pop star, an actress, and was a veterinarian before I was born.

Anyway, don't ask questions about my personal life! It's not your problem. My parents were just kind, smart people who loved animals.

Just like me, so I get it from them.

So there.

Forget it.

I undo his bandage, rub some of the medicine onto him, and look. He is starting to heal!

That is a good sign.

How can he heal so much *that* quickly? I'll have to investigate that. LATER.

I wrap the bandage again.

Then, I hear the *growl*.

The swift brown Texas panther leaps expertly out of the soggy shrubs. The panther sinks its four long sharp canines into Buddy's wounded back. Buddy shrieks in pain and surprise.

No.

Kitty's goin' dowwwwn. Yes. Kitty is the mountain lion.

I take a long, brown, forked branch. I effortlessly try to hit the cougar off. He yowls in pain. He strides majestically and cruelly over to me.

His tongue lolls out. The cougar lets out a deep, low growl. He looks famished for juicy, delicious (athletic, healthy, ha ha!) Riley Meat as drool drips down his fang-filled mouth.

Uh-oh.

He leaps and bites my leg viciously. I howl in agony. "OOOOWWWW!!!!!!!!!!!!!!" I scream. I sound like a wounded ostrich. "You..... Stupid, brainless, foolish, lunatic, overgrown *house* cat!!!!" I yell.

I curse under my breath.

Blood is seeping through my poor foot. My blood-red toes are painful and hurting.

Now I'm going to get an infection from this monster bite.

Terrific.

I will have to wear a leg brace and have a walker and have a cane and be basically an old man.

I have cougar wounds, and Buddy has cougar wounds.

Huzzah. Mazel tov. *Terr*-ific. Cor

"Brainless brainless stupid dumb cat... lunatic, maggot faced son of a warthog. I don't mean you, Ares or Mars," I mutter. *"Dumb cat. Stupid freakshow cat. Humph. What the heck was he trying to do to me? What a walking moron."*

I rip up another piece of my shirt and tie it around my terrifying and searing wound as the cougar *proudly* pads away.

PROUDLY!!!!

In the next few hours, we look for a way to get out of the dark, dense forest, and back home, to our mansion. My muscles hurt intensely and now I have to walk a long way home with joint pain.

I think I have a bone spur or something.

How could this day get any worse?!

My foot hurts like a fire burning through the vein, bone through bone. Buddy helps me over.

Ouch.

Intense.

I feel thorns popping out of my legs. Finally, I see my house. Home sweet home.

I smile.

I want to run through my door, ignoring my relentless agony, swing my door open to find my parents. I want to say, "I'm finally home. Where I belong."

I want to hug my parents so tight, I will never be able to leave again if somebody ever made me.

But then I realize, nope. I can't do that. My parents are dead. A disappointed look appears on my face.

Loss is more painful than any cougar bite.

Because the death of my loving, caring parents hits me with sticks and stones who might break my ribs right where it hurts.

My heart. (Even though it is beyond your ribs, mahn. Sorry, practicing my Jamaican accent, mahn.)

I'm going crazy and over dramatic.

Even though I am partly sobbing right now, that is *only* 'cause I'm an extrovert!!!!!

Wait, am I an extrovert? Who cares!

I'll just get home without much emotion at all.

I shake my head.

See? It works. No crying for *you*. Or me.

Never mind that.

Anna, our maid, is sitting on a nearby chair, knitting a little purple sweater. I wonder who it's for? I bet it's too small for me. It wouldn't even fit my puppy dog General Puppy. DUH. I remember once, Mom put in a wet dress in the dryer, and accidentally pressed fluff and tumble, while talking to me, and when it came out, it could only fit my little toy doll I carried around everywhere. I was just 5 at the time.

"I heard your parents died, my dear Riley. What a tragedy! They must've died painfully!" Anna says, dramatically.

TOO dramatic..!

"Yeah... I'm exhausted." I tell her.

But then, I hear her mumble, "Perhaps I'll take you as my daughter."

"Seriously?" I say.

She ignores me. "We should have a funeral! What a great way to honor them!"

I listen, and ignore her rudeness of mentioning a funeral, (um, MANNERS!) and getting straight to organizing my supervision. I also don't believe a word she just says.

"Are you even listening? I am your mother, now! You must obey me!" she confirms. She snaps out of the dramatic Anna.

"That's not how mothers work!" I tell her. But she doesn't care, nor listens. She clearly isn't a good mother, anyway.

No way José.

SHE IS NOT A MOM.

WHAT MOTHER STARTS TALKING ABOUT FUNERALS *HAPPILY*!?!?!?!?!?!?!?!?!?

She is only meant to be a maid. *My* maid. No good for anything else, especially a *mom*.

"Maybe you won't listen to *me*, but... I don't believe that's a law for old *maids* to turn into mothers. I mean, unless you lie, but if you do, I could tell the authorities on you. You could be shot, an extremely NOT 'pleasant' death. I believe that--" As soon as I am about to finish my lecture on

41

why Anna absolutely shouldn't be my mom, she cuts me off, slapping her long, slender fingers over my mouth.

She tastes like rose perfume. I lick her hand and circle it around and around like a merry go round.

Heh heh.

"*Haha*, Riley, don't be like that! That's not a cause of guns, and let me assure you, this is quite legal. Legal as being able to be alive!"

I roll my eyes at her complete misunderstanding. I am totally devastated! She can't imagine the unbelievable misery I am going through! "*That back pain, Riley! She's just a dummy little girl*," I hear her mumble hatefully. HOW DARE ANNA SAY THAT?!? Okay. I am going waaaaay too strong about it.

"Um, EXCUSE ME?! I'm no dummy, and I don't know if you've noticed, but I'm 13! And anyway, you're the real dummy. You thought I wouldn't hear that, you DUMMY! You're way more than that, you... are...a.... I dunno! Uptight, pain-in-the-neck, ugly, stupid dummy! You're so mean and wretched, and I'm no back pain, thank you very much," I confront, no, snap, very loudly. Very impatient.

She almost explodes in rage. Her face is red, eyes bulging, veins swelling.

I can literally see steam coming out of her ears and nose.

SO WHAT.

"I'll go to my room," I tell her. "If that's what you want."

"If you don't want to, watch TV," Anna says. "I don't care about you."

Goody Goody Gumdrops.

So I do. I watch my favorite movie. My TV is HUGE. It is bigger than those in the movie theaters. I microwave the buttered popcorn and sit down to watch. I like it when the dogs lock up the bad guy.

Then I get tired and eat a slice of cake from the refrigerator.

Next, I play on my viola for practice.

C string or G string? I don't know! I think, stressfully.

After a while, I decide that it's a G string and start playing. I hum to the melodic sound of the bow rubbing against the strings.

"Hm hm hmhm hm hmhmhmhmmm..." I sing, and add some lyrics.

"The mean va-ampires took away my paaa-arents. Now I have to be raised byyy my weird mai-ai-aid. La-la-laaa-la la-la-laa-la-la la-la-la-laaa-la-laaaa-la-la." I laugh so hard after I am done.

It is a parody of the "Ode To Joy" (Beethoven's Ninth Symphony).

I'm not really making fun of it.

I'm just a clever person. And quite creative.

So there.

Then, I play a game with my dog, General Puppy. It's quite a mouthful, so I call him Gen Pup. Gen Puppy, General Pup, Or GP. You name it! He is a brown mastiff puppy with a black muzzle and has a white patch of fur on only one eye. His muzzle is super wrinkly, kinda like a loose bag. A living bag. He's small, but wait till he's larger.

He has floppy ears that go down to his big, bright and encouraging smile. General Puppy isn't ugly. He's cugly! (Cute + Ugly. BAD HABIT! RILEY! STOP JOINING WORDS! Can't help it.) He loves to play with sticks and balls and toy mice.

I think he's half cat. No. Then why would he chase cats? He's not scared of cats either. He has a troublemaking spot for cats. If General Puppy sees a cat and you're walking

44

him, you're *doomed*. He shoots off like a rocket and chases the cat, his tongue lolling out. Last time, when General Puppy chased a cat, you shoulda seen his face and the cat's.

The cat's: Terrified and eyes wide.

General Puppy: Happy, mischievous, and guilty when I scolded him.

We had to give FIFTY dollars to the owner just to say "SORRY. My new dog has a habit of chasing cats."

I found out the hard way.

General Puppy hates vacuum cleaners. If he sees or hears one, or even senses one, he freezes in his tracks and barks like CRAZY!!! He is so afraid of them, that I need a dustpan and broom to clean. I have chores. It's not like only rich kids don't do chores.

Fancy Pants Ugly Higginbottoms, for example. But that's not her real name.

That spoiled brat *should* do tons of chores. She deserves it. She has NO chores.

General Puppy yips and yaps as if he says, *"Yay! <Yip!> What are you waiting for? Throw the ball! Throw it! <Ruff!> <Ruff!> Throw it! <RUFF!! ARF!!>"* I play with him for hours. Then I lie down with my head on General Puppy's belly as a pillow.

"C'mon, boy, let's have some fun outside!" I say. He whimpers.

"Okay, lazy guy. You don't need to go outside." Then I rub his stomach.

"You're so cute," I mumble on the way out the door. I go down the big steps covered in red and gold mats. My parents had gotten them from one of their most rich friends.

"I guess you are having a hard time adjusting to the new plans, Riley. Don't worry, you'll get used to it," Anna says, not so comforting as anticipated. She's reading the book _Dracula._

She has an interest in books like those kinds of stuff.

'_Whatever._' I think, '_Just walk away and pretend you can't hear her._' Unfortunately, Anna knows when somebody's ignoring her, and she doesn't like it _at all._

"Riley, you listen to me now! Having good manners is part of leading a decent life, and I'd like you to do so! Don't be rude to me for caring. As I was saying, I think that you will get used to this new life quickly. You may move out of this mansion with me, a fresh start begins!"

WHAT??!!

No, she can't do these arrangements so soon! My parents' death was only last night! It's like she was planning the whole thing. How did she know in the first place that this whole conundrum started?

I groan.

"Nope. We can decide to move in, like, seven months, but not now! I know, I know. You're the adult here, but *I'm* the one who knows my mom and dad best. They'd decide to plan this later," I confront, testily.

"I'm thinking about it, Riley. Just thinking about it," Anna says.

"Okay, but I want answers tomorrow!" I say, like I'm a head detective asking for answers.

Anna just shakes her head and rolls her eyes.

Humph.

So, apparently Anna doesn't have any manners at all.

"I'll be in the pool if you need me," I say, walking over to my backyard. There's a big private pool and a hot tub in my backyard. I grab my mustard colored bathing suit. Then, "CANNONBAAAAAALL!!!!" I scream, scrunching my legs and body into a hedgehog-like pose, and tying my hands around my bare shins.

I splash into the deep, rippled water.

"Woo-hooo!!!!" I cry.

I float in the water and do a backstroke. I jump on the diving board again. "Yay!!!!" After that, I just relax, float in the water and think about my life. *'I really don't want to move, but... wait! The other day, Mom was just talking about moving! Did she know?'*

That is *weird*.

Was that really related in any way?

Who cares?

I play in my pool for hours.

My cougar wound still stings a bit...

But not much since I put some medicine and some of that spray which makes your wound sting a lot.

But it helps, thank goodness.

I mean like, what if the spray wasn't even invented? Then I'd have a hurtful infection and I'd have to amputate it and I'd have a prosthetic leg and I wouldn't be in the Olympics. Aaand I wouldn't want that, thank you very much.

"Riley! Riley! Time for dinner!" Anna calls from inside my mansion.

"Wait! Thirty more minutes! You're not my mom! I can do whatever I want! My mom lets me eat dinner at any time! So there!" I holler back.

"Fine! But don't tell me I didn't warn you when the hot, creamy pasta gets cold!" She yells back.

Humph.

I wasn't planning on eating dinner tonight, anyway.

I was too busy figuring something out.

Why are these things happening? They seem related.

I've *got* to get to the bottom of this. And soon, before something else unexpected happens!

Tonight after dinner, I have the craziest dream! It's more like a vision, as if it's going to happen, but this vision is crazy! It's not gonna ever even happen. Here.

A winged horse and I are flying over another world. A world that isn't even Earth! There are colossal buildings that look like temples from Ancient Rome! There are people but they are wearing tunics and robes. The green grass is lush and is alive. The world is filled with chatter from tweeting little songbirds. The butterflies are the size of cars!

Weird.

But the most surprising thing is the winged horse! He looks just like Buddy. Same hazel eyes, same white pearly coat. He says something but I just can't figure out the gibberish words. I only catch 2 words, "Anna," and "Vampire."

When I slip and start to fall down off of the winged stallion, I go to a place of dark, lava- filled carven, I step onto the lava! The magma sucks me up! I wake up just as the lava sucks me up whole!

I am drenched with sweat and I'm panting as if I had been running for my life!
This is weird! First weird, then weirder, now weird*est!*

For almost fourteen days (two weeks) I keep getting this odd vision. Is Buddy trying to tell me something?
Nah.
How come horses are magic?
This is crazy.
Wait, is it sent by the vampires? Maybe the dreadful, parent killing vam*poop*ires! Yeah! Vampoopires! Yeah! Maybe they know that I escaped and they want me to be scared to death!
I won't be like that.
Maybe.

Ring! Ring! The alarm clock jolts me awake.
"Huh? What year is it?" I ask, and I laugh. I like going to Home Depot and just running around everywhere,

popping up from the door displays, or hiding behind some plants in the gardening section saying "Hello! What planet are we on? Is it Mars???" and people give me weird looks. Then they realize I'm Riley Peterson.

I stretch before hopping out of my big, light turquoise canopy bed, brushing my teeth and changing into a blue T-shirt with a sparkling sequin pattern forming into a silhouette of a galloping horse. I grin at the horse. My grin is wide, with a little window for one of my teeth I lost. I run down the steps two at a time and smell pancakes and syrup!

"Yummers!" I smile.

I wolf down the stack of delicious pancakes. I eat some fresh cantaloupe, too. I rush up the stairs, select my favorite book and snuggle in my beanbag, drifting into the story. I feel like I'm *in* the book. I am in the mood for that story.

Galloping mooing cows stampede next to my tired body. <Clop, Clop, Clop>. It's almost dawn, and I'm racing free. Dust hits my face. The hooves of my wild horse are growing louder by the minute. My heels kick him. The wind sputters on my messy hair. Coyotes howl early in the morning. We race away without stopping.

51

"Giddy-up! Giddy-up! Ride away!" Shouts one cowboy. I sit up tall with posture and gallop on my American Paint Horse and disappear into the stampede of bellowing cattle. I lasso my rope and single out the leader of the cows. The stocky bull charges through but I snap the rope tight onto his horns and the bull buckles and falls. The cows stop and steer in another direction. My horse and I kick up clouds of dry, muddy sand. I squeeze the sides of my charging horse and yell orders to my cow hands. "Surround the cows! Put 'em into the pasture!" The cow hands listen and the cows are finally in the pasture.

I dismount my exhausted horse. "Here boy, here." I lead him to the water trough and let him have a long, cooling drink. I guzzle water from my canteen. He laps it all up in one long, cold sip. I had a nice drink, too. The fresh water soothes my parched tongue and throat. "What you boys did is a good job. I hope to see it happen again." I walk over to the resting bull. I hold his curvy horns and hand him over to this guy who wants to buy him.

"Good boy, Big Grump, I'll miss you," as I hand him over to the buyer. "Gimme 5 dollars, that's part of the deal." I say.

The man gruffly hands over the money.

I snap the book shut. I just finished a small part. It is a pretty long book, but is still awesome. The bull's for 5 dollars, because it's the old times. 5 dollars would last me a whole month of hay. I mean, the cowgirl. Not me. I rise from my turquoise bean bag. This book is awesome! I'll be an author when I grow up. Or maybe President. Or maybe both. A president who writes books. I love books and stuff about the world and politics. I close my eyes to take a little rest.

"Oh, my word!!!!!" I hear Anna cry from downstairs. I race down the big steps, THREE at a time, trying to figure out what happened.

"WHAT THE *HECK!?!?*"

"I-it's...you...! Riley!!" Anna smiles nervously, her fangs showing.

"Why are you *melting?!*" I ask, not exactly meaning to be rude.

Okay.

Maybe a *little* meaning to be rude.

Heh heh.

"Oh! It's just the sun. It's so hot out today, right?" She asks, and closes the curtains shut.

"Not *that* hot out!! Of course it's warm, but to the point where you melt?! I don't think so. It's not even 90 degrees!" I yell. She's seriously and literally melting like a big, green, jiggly blob of Jell-O! But all of a sudden, venomous sharp teeth pop out of her mouth! She stops melting, and she goes back to normal, but she still has those teeth. And creepy, hollow black eyes. With no white parts. It'll give me nightmares. My neck is throbbing with tension.

She walks slowly closer to me. Her mouth opens up, so her fangs are more visible. Green goop oozes out of her gums. Her mouth opens wider to me, and then... <Chomp!> "AAAAAGGGGHHHHH!!!!!" My sparkly eyes jolt open widely. "Aaaagggghhhh!!!!!!!!!...I scream softly. I was dreaming, fortunately. I wonder what that terrifying dream meant! All signs of vampires... Maybe I'm just afraid. Probably..?

I tip toe out of my room and check on Anna. She's on her black phone.

"Hi Riley, haven't seen you since morning," she grumbles without looking up, and forces her teeth to open.. She is a bit smaller than before, like an inch or two. She is a lot more skinny than this morning.

Weird.

Her teeth have a greenish *tint*. Hmmmm........... Something's *fishy*. And I think I know *why* and *what*.

"GOOOOAAAALLLL!!!!!!!" I cheer. The soccer ball soars through the air. It lands into the net.

Bella grins. "Yeah."

We both are drenched with sweat and my soccer cleats are not working so well with tufts of green grass. All the friction makes it way too hard. Although I love Bella and soccer, my mind is replaying the vision—the dream. Which is really distracting me from doing anything like this. This is the first goal I've made since the past three hours! This is the score.

Bella: 30 goals
Me: 1 goal

I sprint, but I slip since my stupid cleats are not working. *Humph.* I pick out the tufts of grass.

"I really need new cleats. These are as useless as rodents." I grumble.

"But they can be normal shoes, since the spikes are gone." Bella encourages me.

Here's the thing. Bella has a good side for anything, even dying.

An example:

Me: "Help! Bella! I am dying!"

Bella: "Well, at least your life will be at peace. Me no gonna help you."

See what I mean?

I rise and brush myself off. I then run as fast as I can with useless soccer cleats and kick the ball into the goal. I slip; I fall.

I wince.

I flop down onto the soft grass. The timer goes off. *Beep beep beep!*

I sigh.

"What's wrong? You don't seem like yourself." Bella seems concerned.

"I-I had a bad dream," I blurt out.

No way could I tell her about my visions. She'd think I'm crazy and then we would have a life-long pretend sister feud!

I wouldn't want that.

"Well, at least it wasn't a nightmare!" Bella smiles hopefully.

Ugh.

"Hey, we could go to your house. What's your mom making?" I change the subject.

"Oh. Pasta. And Steph is still...well, she still listens to heavy metal. It's annoying. She barely comes to dinner and barely even comes out of her boring room.

"The last time I saw Steph was three days ago. Mom has to give her meals through her dog door thing we had before Griffin died," she mumbles, gloomily. Her dog and General Puppy were the thickest of thieves. Really, they teamed up and stole all the doggy obedience school treats.

A frown turns on my highly freckled face. "Really?! *That* long?" I ask, very surprised.

She nods her perfect-model's-head. She has strawberry-blonde curls, with intense freckles. She has high cheekbones, like a model. She has perfectly shaped eyes and perfect eyebrows.

"I know. Ridiculous, right?" She scoffs, kicking the soccer ball out of her way.

She sits down.

"I feel like..." She sighs, without finishing her sentence. I droop in empathy. I don't say anything just in case she wants to finish it.

57

"I feel like my whole life is changing. So is my family! That's the last thing I need at my age. I mean, I'm almost 14, and my parents don't even realize this about me." She rubs her right arm on both of her eyes to clear the gushing tears out of them. I try putting myself into her shoes, but I just can't! My parents have never been divorced.

But they died.

But it doesn't matter!

This moment is supposed to be about Bel. Me being upset for her.

"Don't worry. On the bright side, your mom and dad didn't end up killing each other!" The second I say that, I instantly think: *Uh-oh. Too soon.* But to my surprise, she just starts to giggle. "Yeah. I didn't think of that," says Bella.

"Let's go to my mom's house."

As we get there, I can already hear music blasting from Stephanie's room.

"I prefer classical and R&B, so turn it down, Stephanie!!!!" She yells.

Stephanie just opens the window, rolls her eyes, and scoffs. "You feisty little gremlin! Think you can control me? Ha. Ha."

Bella growls. Like, REALLY viciously. A tiger growling at its prey. The prey getting scared silly and running for its life, only to get caught by the tiger. Dead as a doorknob.

Ms. Hamilton swings her front door open, her face as frantic as if a bear was on her lawn. Her glasses almost slip off her face.

"Oh! Bella. I didn't think you'd be here this early," she says, puzzled.

"What do you expect?" Bella asks.

"Oh, and if it isn't Riley! How are things?" Ms. Hamilton asks. I shrug.

"Good? I don't know," I say.

"Well, let's go! I really want to go inside, I'm sweaty!" Bella lets out a big breath.

"Yeah, Bella's right. Besides, I'm making milkshakes," Ms. Hamilton says, smiling. *Mmmmm...* Ms. Hamilton's milkshakes are the best. They're made with strawberries and chocolate, and some Italian sweets. I forget what it's called.

We both sit at the table inside. Ms. Hamilton serves us dinner, and she sits down, too.

"So, Bella..." she starts.

"Yeah? Wassup?" asks Bella, shoveling a cheeseburger into her mouth. Ms. Hamilton makes burgers too.

"Well! Your father is going to be in town in two weeks, and he said he wanted to come visit us then," she says, though she's frowning. I can understand. They were so mad at each other.

Bella's smile stretches from Texas to the top of the arctic circle. Okay. Not that wide, but you get it. "Dad?! Next week?! Riley, are you hearing this?!" Bella asks, loudly and joyfully. "Yep, I'm hearing this. I'm so happy for you!" I say, happily.

"Riley can come, too, if you want," Ms. Hamilton offers. I didn't even think about this for one second.

"Uh-huh!" I tell her. Bella squeezes me so tightly, I'm gonna choke and die. Suffocating. Jeez, Bel. I know you're super tough, but like, ouch.

"Yay!"

"Boop-dee-dah-da-da-daaaah-bop-boop-beep-boo-bow-doot-doo-dee-doe!!!" Bella scats. She just started that hobby for some reason, but I like it! She's *way* improving!

Then, she starts playing her trumpet.

(She plays it when she is happy.)

I clap.

"Thank you! And thanks again for coming to see my dad with me. For some reason, I have to thank you for that, but, yeah!" she gushes.

"Anytime." I smile.

"Yeah, but I don't get it. He's not your dad. Why'd you get so excited about it?" she asks.

"In a way, he kind of is. You're like family," I tell her. She smiles. She really is like a sister to me.

After I leave their house, it is already 8 o'clock! When in the world did that happen?! I race home, to find who at the doorstep? That's right.

Anna.

"Anna! I can explain why I'm here so late!" I'm so frightened, my voice almost turns to mush. But I sound strong. A little. Fine. Not a bit.

Hands on hips, frown on face, furrowed eyebrows, she's all ready to punish me.

"What makes you think that you can stay up so late, Riley? You forgot to take out the garbage!"Anna yells, angrily. She points up the stairs.

"Into your room. NOW!" She orders like my mom when she grounded me. I sulk up to my bedroom, lie down, thinking about how much better off people would be if magic were real. I look out my window, finding Buddy sleeping right in his stable. I slouch down and rest my chin on my palms.

I sigh.

'*Sometimes I wish you were magic, Buddy,*' I think and lay my head on my pillow to rest. Then, I realize that I can stand up to Anna, The Worst Witch-Faced Maid Ever!

I race down the stairs, thinking about what to say to Anna. Then, she looks at me. She opens her mouth to talk, but then I interrupt her by blurting out what I call a good 'stand-up'.

"Anna! I am not your real daughter. Don't you dare boss me around or I could fire you. You are still like a maid to me. I don't have as many chores as my real parents told me I don't. I could tell the authorities on you any time I need to and you could be shot or put in prison," I bark.

"No way. I have permission to do whatever I please." Anna fumes.

I storm off and fake call the authorities.

"I'm calling the coppers!!!" I cover my hand over my mouth, trying to stash away my unstoppable giggles. Coppers are what Karen, my viola teacher, calls the cops.

Anna looks like she saw a ghost.

"Okay, okay, I won't boss you around or give you too many chores but don't call the police. Please."

Ha.

I won.

Her nose scrunches up like she's a kid again. "But I believe that you are to be in your room. Please. Go. Now!" she scolds as I run up and turn off the lights.

"What a bossy woman," I grumble under my breath.

The dark is beautiful inside my nice bedroom. I come back under my windowsill, and watch the glowing stars in the dark night sky.

Soaring helicopters glide noisily in midair. While I'm stuck in here because a rude maid sent me to this dungeon! Well, it's not really a dungeon, but with Anna telling me to come here?

Total. Dungeon.

I look at my adorable Buddy boy, sleeping the night away. It looks like he's snoring.

That reminds me, *I* should get some rest. I yawn and stretch my arms out. I watch my ceiling vigorously until I'm hypnotized and deeply asleep, in the magical place of Dreamland. Or maybe even Nightmareland.

Ugh.

Chapter Three

You Don't Believe It. *I* Don't Believe It. I Musta Hit My Head

Two days later, 8:00 AM

I flop down on my bed.

"What should I do?" I wonder, quietly. I feel so alone!

Of course I still have my Buddy! But my parents are dead. Anna Ying, my so-called-trusty maid, decided to make me her adopted daughter. It's kinda weird being an orphan, but, I guess I could survive!

Anna is Chinese American, and I am American and Greek and Belgian and Polish and Czech and Italian and German and Brazilian and a lotta other stuff (I'm a mutt.) so it kind of looks weird seeing us stand together.

She wears different clothing. She always wears a gothic long black dress with a gothic long blouse and a pink flower hairpin. So many 'OW' sounds, huh?

AAAAAAWOOOOOOOO!!!!!!!!!!!!!!!!!!!!!!!!!!!!!!!!

I'm part wolf.

Anna combs her short hair so it's straight and even. My hair, on the other hand? I would brush my hair for an entire century, and not a single strand would be smooth enough or slick and straight.

My hair is a little wavy, (NOT CURLY) and is very tangled....Hehe. She has a different 'surname' than me. That's what she calls it. Surname. I call it 'last name.'

I have really dark brown hair with no bangs with streaks of blonde hair and *SHE? She* has hair black with bangs, she uses a LOT of makeup. No *wonder* she sweats even in the winter. (I only use sparkly blue-raspberry flavored lip gloss here and there.)

Plus her teeth look kind of like a vampire's teeth! Wait—is that even a trait? I hope so! It should not be real vampire teeth. The point is, we don't look like a real family.

I go to my bookshelf, grab a thick copy of the Roman Myths, and start to read. I carefully turn the fragile, brown, acid-covered pages. I turn straight to the page how Pegasus, The Winged Stallion of Olympus, was born. Pegasus sounds so awesome, and magnificent, even! He is breathtaking! He is so majestic and regal and adventurous.

"Pegasus was born when the Olympian hero, Perseus, beheaded Medusa, the Gorgon. He sprang out of her severed neck along with his brother Chrysaor. Another hero, Bellerophon took his bridle and controlled Pegasus," I read out loud. Where are the heroines, like Atalanta?

Pegasus sounds so good. "I wish Pegasus was here," I blurt out. Suddenly, a flash of glitter and yellow bursts through the air, and knocks me onto my bed. Hard. There is Buddy. With wings! He is soaring through the air in a blinding light. *'No, I'm just daydreaming.'* I think, *'Snap out of it, Riley, I'm just gonna go back to this book.'* but, no. I'm not daydreaming. I look at my book. Pegasus is still there! But he lives in Olympus! ... Or does he?

"No. It can't be!" I blurt.

But here he is!

Buddy with his collar made of sparkling diamonds, and his pearly white coat. And WINGS! IT CAN'T BE! OMG! My eyes nearly pop out of my head! I have Pegasus as my very own pet! He looks a bit different than Buddy. First of all, he has those wings. Duh! He has hazel eyes. But in those eyes, if I look VERY closely, I can see him flying in the air. His tail is flowing to the floor.

"I have been waiting for you to turn me into Pegasus," says Pegasus, formally.

"I must have hit my head, or something!" I scream, denying what I'm seeing at this second. I stroke his wings. "Even your coat doesn't feel real!" I add, smiling ear to ear.

"Yes, for I am a mythical creature, yes, yes." He tells me, grinning proudly.

"Can you be my sidekick? I need loads of help. Mystery stuff. You know, girl stuff," I tell him, still all smiles.

"What shall I help you with?" he asks.

I tell him the whole vampire thing, as he listens very intently. He tells me that he remembered seeing it all in action. He says he remembers the lady with the Victorian Dress, and how the vampires choked and strangled my dad, and how Dracula [rudely] told my mom to 'zut up.' He rambles on and on about his battles. "The vampires... Yes. I have been battling that vampire clan for eons! Eons!" he booms. "Finally, you, Riley, will help me with my war!"

I laugh. "Of course I would. You are my best friend!"

I beam broadly.

Knowing that Pegasus was now my friend is *the best feeling in the universe!* "You can be it for as long as you like too. Bestie," I offer. A great opportunity to be friends with

67

magic. He smiles under his chin. He proudly struts around the room. He knocks over everything! Ugh! I had just redecorated my room a day ago!

A few minutes later, we two are sitting on our own private lawn. Anna or the other maids, cooks, butlers, tutors or anyone else don't know where it is.

It is perfect.

"Pegasus, what is it like on Olympus?" I ask.

I've been bombarding Pegasus with questions for hours. Okay, not hours. We had to tip-toe out of the room, avoid Anna, and make sure anyone didn't see Pegasus. If anyone did, then BOOM! Word would get around and soon the paparazzi would be chasing us! <clicking camera sound effect. Repeat 100,000,000 times.>

That would be *horrible*.

"It never rains but the flowers always bloom. The breeze is calm and is never ever polluted. The butterflies are the size of cars. No one is homeless and everyone is plenty rich. Jupiter's palace is magnificent and huge. You sleep on canopy beds. You get ambrosia for food. It is like honey but more like nectar," he explains.

"Pegasus? What is Juno like?" I ask curiously.

"She is very nice. She may have a fit if Jupiter doesn't give her what she wants. Juno having a fit is like taking over the planet."

I giggle. Juno has a temper? "The Sphinx is her most favorite guard on Olympus. Juno wears a long silky robe woven with gleaming pearls. Her hair is done. She has an olive wreath in her brown-blonde hair," Pegasus says.

"Wow! She sounds beautiful!" I say, mesmerized.

"That is how Juno is." Pegasus chuckles.

"Pegasus, how are Neptune's horses like?" I ask.

"Neptune's horses have fish tails for back legs. They can gallop only when there is water on the ground. So Neptune puts in a pool of water so that they move," Pegasus says. I interrupt him and say beaming, "A kiddie pool!"

Pegasus grins and says, "Yes, yes, a kiddie pool."

"How are Pluto's horses?" I ask.

"Pluto's horses are skeleton horses that scream hideously and they have to be blindfolded since they can't stand the sunlit world. They are used to the dark underworld." Pegasus shudders. "I never play with his horses but I do with Jupiter and Neptune's since Neptune's are my brothers and Jupiter's are my cousins. Pluto's are also my

69

cousins too, but they are too scary," he says. He shudders again.

"Ok Pegasus. We could go downtown to the park where horses are allowed," I say.

"Sure." Pegasus says.

We are at a horse park/paddock. Buddy is now Buddy, a horse. We play tag with other horses. A Morgan Horse named Bailey becomes his friend. They play tag. Buddy's now it. He gallops toward another horse and gently nips the horse; Bailey bucks. She neighs gleefully and races everywhere. Then, she stomps her left front hoof on a Lustino horse named Summer. Summer gives a stern look at Bailey. Summer isn't really the playing kind of horse. She just stands there, watching. Bailey whinnies and steps on Summer's hoof again. Summer huffs and then she looks at Bailey as if to say, "Never do that again." Bailey runs around again and knocks me down. "Woah, you're strong!" I say to Bailey. She kind of smiles at me. Buddy kicks Bailey on her butt. "Buddy!" I scold, "Don't do that." They play there for hours. When we come back home, I watch a movie....play a video game.....and play a board game. It really is a bored game..............and take a nap. Buddy does, too. We are both worn out. *Snooooore........* Buddy snores.

I wake up, bored as a brick wall. "Uuuugh..." I moan, quietly, so that I won't wake Buddy up. I look at our mailbox.

'Maybe I'll get the mail,' I think. I open the mailbox. *'Taxes for dad... taxes for mom... heh. They don't know that they're dead.'* But then, I find an actually *important* letter from... *Drake Banis?* Who in the world is Drake Banis?

I open it slowly. Who is this man? I keep wondering. *Why would he be writing to us? Probably fan mail. Mom was a model. After all...*

It reads:

We will haunt thee, we will taunt thee for the rest of thou life!

Thy will live

In fear and misery, dread and despair. Always will we

break one piece of

Thou heart,

Until it is all gone!

Wow. That is provoking. I throw it in the trash, but I'm still quite concerned. "Hmmm... I don't understand this letter," I say, out loud. "They will haunt me and taunt me,

71

but the ending is confusing, 'Always will we break one piece of thou heart, until it is all gone'? 'All gone'? Interesting." What would that mean? Oh! I get it! Oh no! That means that they will haunt me for my entire life and they will take one part from my heart and take it away until I die and then I'll be dead! But, metaphorically or literally?

I turn Buddy back into Pegasus. "I wish that Pegasus was here--" Before I even put a stop to my sentence, he magically appears. "What do you need me for.......<*Yaaawwwnn*>?" Asks Pegasus, half asleep. "Listen, Bud. I wanna show you something I found in the mailbox. Look," I say. And then I run back to the trash and fish out the letter. Blegh! It has white bird poop on it- plus General Puppy's warm, squishy dog poop.

"How'd it get so dirty and so quickly?!" I say, disgusted.

Never mind.

I run back to Pegsy. "Look! The letter."

I wave the stinking letter. Poop flies everywhere. I duck down. "Some guy sent it. It says:

We will haunt thee, we will taunt thee for the rest of thou life! Thy will live

In fear and misery, dread and despair. Always will we break one piece of

Thou heart, until it is all gone!"

I shiver visibly. I hate this Drake to my toes.

I *hate* him!

"We have to burn Drake—He really is Dracula (I can tell by how formal his writing is and how his handwriting is)--to ash. Or you will die. But wait! I have powers. I may as well stop this curse," Pegsy says.

Dracula?

Then I hear him mumble something in another language. Olympian, perhaps?

All of a sudden, there is a flash of yellow glittery light and the words on the letter change!

It now says:

We will not bother you at all.

Are we ever to bother you,

Only in dreadful, horrible nightmares twice-thrice a month.

73

156 times a long, long year!
We will not bother you,
You, the curse, have lifted. And,
Only a midst of the curse is there.

(Wait... *thrice?* Is that some weird vampire number?)

I breathe a sigh of relief. The curse is lifted!

But a midst of the curse?

What?

Oh!

The nightmares. 156 times a year! I HATE NIGHTMARES. Especially vampires.

Real vampires.

Who gets inside my dreams?... Wait an earth second, how would they do that?

Get in my own, personal brain and top secret, private thoughts? Are vampires able to do that?

It'd be pretty neat if *I* could do that!

I would trick the vampires into dreaming about GARLIC! SUNLIGHT! WOODEN STAKES! Then they'd die.

Ha!

"Pegsy, can you change the curse?" I wondered.

74

"I'm afraid not, since I cannot do such a thing. Anyway, a curse is a curse," he says.

I pout. "But I thought that you had powers," I whine.

"I can alter a curse, but not completely change it, Riley. Be happy with what you have. I have changed all I can," he says.

"Okay.... Why do you have to be like Mom and Dad?" I say.

I feel a pang in my throat mentioning my parents.

My *dead* parents.

Tears prick the back of my eyes. Then, without warning, they spill out.

"Why are you crying? Oh! Your parents!" he says.

I sniff, furiously flicking away drops of salty tears. Pegsy licks my wet cheek, like General Puppy.

His licks are warm, wet, and *slobbery*. General Puppy's are a bit more wet and slobbery. *Okay......* General Puppy's are *waaaay* more wet and slobbery. General Puppy's are like pools of puppy slobber (spit) on my face and Pegsy's are small and neat. I stop crying and look at him. "Pegsy, I never knew that you licked people," I say.

"So what!" he says and takes another lick.

Humph.

The next day I go on another ride on Pegsy. He has finally agreed to fly with me. But only in the black of the night. I wait until it is 1:54 AM so that Anna is asleep and that no one will notice us in the dead of night.

I go to the stables as I quickly say the words to turn Buddy into Pegsy. There is a flash of yellow and Pegsy's there.

It's time.

I get onto his back and he gallops faster than the cool night breeze and lifts off into the air.

I whoop with absolute joy! I feel so...*tiny*, under the colossal sea of twinkling stars.

"This is totally rad!" I scream with happiness.

"Yes! This is fun, but I am a bit bored of the flying, since on my home Olympus, this hovering roller coaster of 'fun' is more like a routine. There are more winged horses in Olymp—" he says, but I interrupt him by saying, "More winged horses?!"

"Yes, more winged horses. As I was saying, There are a few more winged horses on Olympus but I am _the_ winged

76

stallion of Olympus. I am...son of Neptune, nephew of Jupiter and Pluto, son of Medusa, the Gorgon, snake hair, you-turn-to-stone-if-you-look-at-her-and-her-2-siblings."

'Kaaay?????? Pegasus is the son of Medusa.

"Pegsy....Olympus is the best place in the universe!!!!!" I say.

"Do you want to go....now?" he says, grinning. "I bet you'd love Jupy Jupiter's Palace! Not to mention the fact that my private garden is both of ours and that you could live on Olympus starting tomorrow! We could even bring your puppy!" he says. My jaw drops.

I get to live on Olympus! And bring General Puppy, the cute bundle of trouble!!!

"Sure! Let's go pack and bring General Puppy and my diary," I say, excitedly.

"Actually...... let's do that.......next month??? I'm sure we have to solve this bloodthirsty mystery. You know, girl stuff???" Pegsy repeats what I said when he first turned into Pegasus.

I hang my head, disappointed. I slowly nod.

"Hey, hey, hey, miss...drama queen, quit that sulking. We can go next month," he says. "Fiiiiiiiine," I groan.

Chapter Four

Pure Wild Really *Is* Wild

A Week and Many Letters Later At The Vampire's Haunted Palace

Have you got zee little guhl?" asked the Chief vampire, Dracula.

"Not yet..." Anna responded, carefully. Just about when Dracula was going to swear, Anna cut him off.

"But, sthee is my adoptive jild, now, zee leettle orphan guhl. She has no idea that I'm a vampire! Mwahaha!"

"Ve do not say 'Mwahaha'!" said the count, firmly.

"I know you don't, but that's just a zeettle drama for you," Anna said. Ignoring the count, she continued her report, "And, zees mordning, I saw that stupid horse, Baddy, vas acthually Pigaseesth!"

"Pigaseesth?! Zat zeetle scondrrel??! Ve've VINALLY vound imm!!" cheered Dracula triumphantly with joy, "MWAHAHAHAHA!!" All the vampires at the meeting stared at him. "Are you clueless? You just said you did not say 'Mwahaha'!" Anna pointed out.

"Be garevul vat you zay adround me, or you'll get ZURNED!" said Dracula, boiling in rage.

"Yes, sorrdy, masteer." Anna lowered her head in shame. " Ve vill kill Pigaseesth so that his planz vill be gone! Ve vill rule Olymups!!"

Dracula looked at the sea of stars where the portal to the world of Olympus probably was. He cackled, " Vonce Pigaseesth eez dead, ve vill rule over all ov Olymups!!! That's eet. Ve vill vin vair and squvare!!" He threw back his head and howled into the moonless night. "Haaaa HAAAA!!!!!!!"

Splash! Splash! Splash! I ride my black Frisian horse under the magnificent waterfall. AAAAhhhh. Water splashes playfully over my long flowing white dress. Starry Night, the Frisian horse's long, feathered hooves splash water onto my face. I laugh. I spot a beautiful peacock on the slippery rocks. I love it here! I see lush trees and woodland. The rocks are covered in bits of moss. The water gushes and swirls around rocks in the waterfall's path. This is paradise. The water is the color of tropical sea green emeralds and has no pollution.

I'm spreading my arms out as the water tickles my outstretched hands. The water feels...silky smooth like feathers. I start to mount Starry Night when—

"Riley! It's me! Bella! Wanna go out for ice cream with our horses? We could get two cones each! One for our horses and one for us." Bella is out of breath when she scrambles up the grand staircase.

A golden chandelier with shiny diamonds encrusted in it, sparkles.

I rise from my beanbag, holding a book. I'm a bookworm.

"Of course! Anna! I'm going out for ice cream!" I yell.

"Sure!" Anna's nose is stuck in her black *bat* phone.

Weird.

I bet she's watching some dumb—and totally not funny-videos.

We rush down the stairs, two at a time. I look up to my domed, glass ceiling.

We rush out the door and I tack Buddy up. I hope I don't turn him into Pegsy.

Surely, I won't.

Right?

Right.

We gallop quickly over to Frank's Chillin' Ice Cream shop.

I order a strawberry and chocolate ice cream with whipped cream and extra rainbow-flavored sprinkles. Plus a cherry.

I get some carrots and double cherries for Buddy.

Bella on the other hand, well she got vanilla and pistachio for her horse, Sergeant.

Seriously! Ice cream! I feed Buddy the carrots and the two red cherries.

I then enjoy my icy and creamy ice cream.

I savor the dripping cream.

I then gobble up the crunchy cone.

Mmmm............... Then my stomach rumbles and churns. Oh right. I forgot about my pills.

Bella smiles as she remembers something.

"Hey Ri, wanna, mmm.....go to the ranch nearby? I'm sure Sergeant would love it since he was born there. He was raised by his dam, Princess. His sire was Midnight. I bet he'd love to see Rambunctious, the German Shepherd dog."

We are trotting over to Rambunctious's Ranch.

Huh.

They named it after a dog?

81

Funny.

I glance at Bella, who is all smiles.

We enter the ranch and get slobbery licks from a big, burly dog.

The German Shepherd, I suppose. "Aahhh!! Dog attack! Ahh!!!!" I almost scream but I absolutely do *not* want to wake up any cute dozing horses or startle any wild, crazy horses.

I see an old guy walk up to my terrified self.

Stranger danger?

My face is at the verge of melting in fear as the huge dog takes a lick for my nose.

The stranger walks up to me.

"Don't worry! This is Rambunctious! The famous dog who named this ranch," Bella assures, laughing heartily.

Bella ruffles the dog's hair playfully.

"Not funny," I say, my teeth clenched together.

I glance at the guy. He picks up my hand and attempts to help pick me up. He holds it out to shake my hand, once I get up. I shake his hand politely.

"Bella! My niece!" The man embraces her tightly.

"How's Stephanie? I heard she's not handling the divorce. My sister told me. I mean, my sister is your mom and moms know what's going on." The man chuckles nervously. He has a stereotypical southern farmer accent.

"Uncle Roger! Ummm.... yeah so this is Riley, my BFF." Bella nods. Her full-teeth smile is showing again. It's totally contagious!

So, like any contagious thing, I smile, too.

"Hey, wanna hear a sick joke? What was the frog's grade? *Toad*ally a minus B!" I crack up like an egg. (Yes, I like bad jokes. They are so corny.) Bella winces. "Toadally bad."

"You seem like delightful friends. Why don't you stay a while?" he asks.

"We'd love to." I giggle.

He looks at me. "You're Riley, correct?" he asks.

I shake his hand again. "Riley Peterson, at your service."

He laughs, "Well, this ranch is welcome to big and small, and especially tall." He says, patting a horse's back. The horse whinnies.

I grin.

Ranches and stables always make me feel better if I'm upset. I'm not, but it's still cool to be there.

"You can call me Roger," the man says.

Er, Roger. Before *Roger* even starts a conversation, Bella is off petting *ponies*.

Rambunctious runs to me, jumps up and licks me.

"Aaaggghhh!!!" I yell again.

Roger picks him up.

"Not a dog person, eh?" he asks.

"No, no," I assure, getting up, and dusting my jodhpurs off, "I actually have one at my home. His name's General Puppy. A mastiff puppy. He's not really a big dog yet, so I'm not used to larger ones."

"Ah, I see," he tells me. But I don't think he sees it. He opens his mouth to keep talking, but Bella comes running over, huffing for breath. "I... am pretty sure... we should go now..." She says. When she finally catches her breath, she continues, "I'm kinda bored, anyway. No offense, Uncle Roger."

"None taken." Roger smiles and waves goodbye to us.

Sergeant whinnies as if to protest, *"I haven't seen my mother!"*

"Oh! Yeah! Hey, where's Princess? Bring 'er here," Roger calls to a rancher.

One second later, a beautiful Morgan horse struts up to us, majestically. Sergeant prances up. They look like twins, but Princess is taller. And a girl. And is way older. So, not really twins, but they look a lot like they could be family. (Which they are.) "Also bring Midnight," Roger calls a second time. Ten seconds later, a male brown Arabian horse gallops regally over. Sergeant nickers oh so very happily! Bella smiles. "Aaannnddd......Sergeant's cousin!" Roger cheers. Wow.

A beautiful mare clumsily gallops over. She's an American Paint. She kind of reminds me of the mare in the _Napoleon's Horses_ book.

"Her name's Sierra. She's real sweet. Givin' birth in... 'bout a month."

Wow.

Sergeant has so many relatives. And nephews or nieces, soon!

"I never knew that horses could get so emotionally happy before!" I exclaim.

"And _I've_ never seen this many horses before," Bella tells us, watching a grazing Belgian Warmblood.

I giggle. "Yeah. Me neither!"

Then, Roger brings up another horse.

"This 'un here is Pure Wild. She was from the west of Texas, from a wild herd. All 'er ancestors were wild 'uns.

That scar, on her face. I saw ya lookin' at it. It came from a wolf bite. She has a wild streak. That is the wild streak that Sergeant also has."

"Yup," Bella agrees, nodding. "He has a *pretty* big one."

Pure Wild is this really majestic horse, but she's skinny. She's a white-ish grayish color. And she has a HUGE scar. It stretches all the way from her forehead to her nose, and it looks fresh, or like she got it a week ago. She also has a scar above her hoof. She has scars everywhere. She's a tough cookie.

"She seems like she fought with another horse or something," I say, walking carefully over to her.

"Sure did. The scar, on her cannon, is from a fight. Same with her neck and her hindquarter," Roger says, nodding.

I take a step forward towards Pure Wild, but she pins her velvety, scarred ears back on her mane, giving a warning not to go close to her.

I stand closer to Bella now. Bella doesn't notice me. She's too busy stroking the majestic Midnight.

"I guess Sergeant... really likes it here." Bella looks upset.

"What's wrong, *Amigo?*"   Roger asks Bella. "Well," she hesitates, "I think it'd be best if he stayed with you."

Roger seems really surprised. "No way, my Bella! We can't do that! Sergeant, the lil' rascal, is yours fair and square."

"Yeah, but Sergeant needs a buddy!" Bella almost looks like she's going to cry. That second, right when she says "Buddy" I get an idea.

"Bel! Buddy can be Sergeant's pal!" I say, happily. "Really?" She sniffles.

"Sure he can! The two can have playdates and stuff whenever we meet up, we can even make fun horse activities they can do together! Like obstacle courses! Oh! We can even craft their own little stable they can play together in, too!!! And maybe--" Just then, I just get hit by the most amazing idea in history ever!

"Oh. My. Gosh! What if we start a horse playgroup for our horses?!" Bella's face becomes completely delighted. I'm so happy she likes it!

"Riley, that's like, literally the awesomest idea since the microphone!" She shrieks like a pterodactyl. Pure Wild snorts angrily, startled. "Oops. We'll shriek more quietly." I start, then guffaw, doing a belly laugh.

From the corner of my eye, I see a rancher accidentally lets go of Pure Wild's rope.

Bella sings. "La la la!!!"

Bella *loves* to sing.

I laugh.

"But better!"

"Woah, now, girls. Now, don't get too addicted to doin' that kinda stuff for yer horses. They may not like it, them horses." Roger warns us. Bella loves the idea, so she totally ignores Roger's warning. I do, too, because, I mean, come on, Roger! I'm trying to cheer Bella up!

"Oooh, we can even make a playroom in that stable!" Bella exclaims.

"We can dress them up, too! They'll have sleepovers when we have sleepovers! We can even make them a fancy horse-friendly dinner!" I slap my hand on my cheeks happily.

"Yeeeeees!!!" Bella groans, with joy.

Roger just shakes his head. He walks on over casually to one of the most beautiful ponies I have literally ever witnessed. Bella and I are too busy gushing over my awesome idea to notice until Roger calls us.

"Girls!"

We look over.

The second we see this wonder, we totally forget the horse playgroup!

"How did—Where did you—Aaaaah!" We squeal like injured pigs!

The pony is snow white, with silky hair, pink nose, *yeah*. She has it all.

We look at each other like we both defeated the terribly evil Dracula! Except that Bella knows nothing about this.

"You wanna pet her? She's good," Roger says.

We run over to this magical-looking wonder horse and start putting fake braids in her hair and stroking her fine white coat.

"You're so sweet!" I swoon.

"Woah! She's gotta be, like, a winning pony or something! Right?" Bella asks Roger. "Actually, yes. She won first place at the county fair." Roger shrugs, not interested.

I look amazed.

"What's her name?" Bella asks.

"Doesn't have one. You girls wanna name 'er?" Roger asks, not as excited as he should be.

"Seriously?!" Bella asks, kind of doubting this privilege.

"Yep."

We scream gleefully, and then huddle together like football players and whisper what name we want to pick out for her. "How about Sugar," I suggest. "That would be great because she is sweet, and her coat's white. No joke," I explain.

"Perfect! Sugar it is!" Bella agrees. I brush pretend dust off my shoulder in pride. I have a talent for naming things.

"Sugar," we say to Roger.

"Great. Sugar is a wonderful name for this sweet pony," he agrees. We giggle.

Then, <WHINNY!!!!!!!!!!!!!> Something hits me like a freight train at 1 billion mph in my side!

"Ooooooowwwwwww!!!!!" I howl in agony. I dart my gaze up, to see Pure Wild slamming her dangerous, sharp hooves onto my legs. I moan, rolling on the sandy ground. "Oooowww," I manage to croak out. I vomit a lot of icky pancake mush from today.

Pure Wild is about to slam her forelegs on my face when Buddy steps in the way! Pure Wild rears up, and whinnies in fury. Buddy's nostrils flare angrily as he kicks and he bites viciously like a rabid, wild dingo from Australia.

Pure Wild is finally hauled away by at least ten ranchers.

Roger rushes over, and checks for any wounds. There are *many*. "Are you okay?" he asks frantically.

I shake my head weakly. He tries helping me to stand, but my knees buckle.

I wail, "I think my leg is broken!"

Then everything is black.

Chapter Five

Truth And Injury. Anna! Don't Read My Notes!

I wake up in an unfamiliar place. Beeping gray machines surround me, and tubes are stuck all over me. I think I look like a devil. Or Frankenstein's monster! A tube is stuck to my right arm like I'm missing something in my body that I'm supposed to have.

Blood maybe?

A plastic tank of saline water is attached to my same arm.

"She's awake," an unfamiliar stranger's voice says. His voice is dark. I try seeing who he is but my vision is super blurry.

"Riley, are you awake?" my babysitter Alia asks worriedly. She was my babysitter when I was six! It isn't surprising to see that she is there, since she is a doctor now.

I gurgle out strange, alien-like words, as if I was a little infant learning to speak. I'm trying to say, "I feel like vomiting and I'm sleepy."

"I think you can't speak for a bit, so write," Alia soothes. She hands over a sheet of paper. She hands a pencil too. I FEEL LIKE VOMITING AND I AM SLEEPY. I write in shaky, three- year- old kid handwriting, not the swirling, neat cursive handwriting I usually write in.

"Oh," Alia says softly.

She gives me a plastic bag and I hack and spit out yellow vomit. *Ewww.........* My face is still green like grass and my stomach churns violently like butter being made. She takes the bag and throws it away. Bleh. WHO IS GOING TO PAY FOR THE BILLS? MY PARENTS ARE DEAD FROM A CAR ACCIDENT AND I DON'T WANT TO BE IN FOSTER CARE. I write and sigh. My hand is tired and sore with bruises from the wild mustang. My head is throbbing and dizzy. "Anna is. She is in the waiting room," Alia assures. She tells a nurse in red scrubs to bring Anna here. I doubt she is very happy to pay the bill and she would definitely not be happy with *me*. NO THANKS. I DON'T

REALLY LIKE ANNA THAT MUCH. I write hastily. Anna

comes in, eyes narrowed, her lips scrunched up and sour as if she just licked a tart lemon. Anna is always a sour puss around me, lately. I meet her gaze, and we lock eyes. Anna glares at me daggers. Apparently, she doesn't like paying bills.

I give her the mega bad, extra worse "I'll kill you later when I get better. I swear." stare.

Anna reads my notes. I wish I could speak and tell her, "No! No! Don't read these!" but I can't.

What is wrong with me? I wonder, panicking.

"I don't believe we've discussed this yet," Anna waves the copy paper I'm writing on in my face. I squint at her menacingly, meaning, *I hate you!* "You don't like me?" Anna asks.

I squint again. I strain my neck to get as close to Anna's face as much as I can, but it hurts. I scrunch up my eyebrows, pull up my chin, and pull on my extra deluxe sour face.

94

You disgust me!

"You disgust me?" She smirks.

She cackles and smirks again at me.

Huh?

How does she know what I'm thinking?

"Oh, look at your ridiculous little smug face! Ha! I'm glad I'm leaving this dump." She struts out to the exit like a proud grouse or emu, still laughing her evil, icy heart out. How rude of her! What happened to manners? "You—are—a—rat!" I manage to spit heavily out.

"Hmm?" Alia asks, walking in.

"N-nothing," I murmur.

"Oh, you can speak again! That's great! What a miracle!" Alia clasps her hands together tightly. Her palms grip together for a little bit.

I can only exhale. "Can't... Inhale..." I tell her, my breath raspy.

"Yes, I can believe so," she tells me, handing a paper cup of water to me.

I sip it up.

"That horse probably knocked the wind outta you! After all, your friend Bella has told me what happened. Here, I need to tell you something, though."

I listen closely, straining my neck. Ouch.

"We found your leg is very hurt. It is a little infected," she whispers darkly, as it all comes back to me.

"That cougar! He bit me, too," I tell her, with a quiet tone. I'm panting just from saying that! I'm really sick!

"W-what?!" Alia asks, shockingly. "What bit you?"

"A cougar. Sank his jaws into the same leg."

Her face is screaming!

"Really? Why? How?" she asks, interested.

"That I don't know," I lie.

I don't want her thinking that I'm crazy! I don't tell her about the vampire thing.

"All I can imagine is a blur. I only remember my leg being almost viciously devoured by that wild animal..." I tell her, dramatically.

Alia gasps. "He only bit you, though," she confirms.

"Yeah. I hate my teeth marks, though." I say.

"I got to see someone else right now. Dr. Jones will take over if you need anything."

I nod in understanding.

Another doctor enters the room. Her name is Marie, I think. Alia always calls her that.

"Marie, would you just tell her she has a visitor. One person at a time." Alia leaves the room.

And with that, she leaves just as fast as she said that thing to Marie, or Doctor Jones.

"Riley, someone's here to see you," Marie tells me.

"Hello!" a familiar voice calls. Bella!

I feel like cheering, but my stomach churns.

"Hi," I croak.

"Oh. You can't speak that much. I heard your leg bone shattered in six places. Plus you were out the entire ride in the ambulance and you were still out cold for two days!" Bella's words just tumble out.

"What!?" I shoot straight up like a rod. She acted like I was supposed to know that!

"Two days!?" I am shocked. And my bone shattered in six places?!

"Is there surgery?" I ask nervously. I try to move my leg. I wince. My leg starts throbbing in pain. "Ow ow ow!"

"Are you okay? Anyway, yes, there is surgery and they are gonna put a rod in your leg." Bella shrugs.

WHAT?!

I'm so upset that tears drip down my eyes like a waterfall rushing down a stressful and dangerous stream. My face remains feelingless, though. I stare at a wall behind Bella. "A-are you okay?" Bella asks, concerned. I don't answer. "Riley? Are you okay?" she repeats. My eyes twitch. I let out a gigantic sigh.

"Not really," I finally admit. "I kinda wanna be alone."

She nods understandingly and walks away in slight sorrow.

"Can I walk?" I say to Marie.

"Yes, but you'll need these crutches, and I'll accompany you." She hands me the crutches.

"Thank you!" I smile, forcing my teeth to show and walk off to the exit. We (Marie and I) walk a little far, until we reach a *graveyard.*

I find a grave that reads:

ELLENA PETERSON

WIFE, MOTHER, DAUGHTER

I gasp. *Mom!* I wonder where Dad is, but I only assume he was right next to her.

One of our butlers must have buried them! I think.

I hobble away with my bulky crutches, Marie looking solemn. Weird. Why didn't anyone tell me she was buried? I guess they wanted to keep it a secret. But why? Maybe the butlers would not want me to know.

I re-enter the hospital and settle into my bed. I drift peacefully into the world of the happy dreams. (Just means I fall asleep.)

6 weeks and a lotta letters later... after Riley heals. She can walk now......

As the alarm clock rings, I wake up with pride that my dear pet is Pegasus! I shudder from all those letters from Dracula! I shake the feeling off. I go to look out my window, and Buddy is just his old regular body. He is Buddy, again.

99

"Wait, boy! Where are you?! Where is the real you? Where is Pegasus?" I ask. I TOTALLY forgot how to change Buddy back into Pegsy. I was in the hospital, ya know.

How could he come back? Maybe we have to ask a fairy. Or maybe I have to read the Roman Myths. I hop out of bed, and go over to my bookshelf.

I look everywhere.

NO!

I should say, "Oh, I wish I could see Pegasus!" I am hoping for him to magically transform, somehow. And, my wish comes true! I see a puff of yellow. I run a little bit slowly, because of my stupid injury.

"Peggy! Pegs-y pegs, pegs! Pegasaurus! You're back, Pegasus! You're back," I fool.

I notice the scared look on his pale face.

"Riley! This is no time to celebrate! The vampires! They were on my tail! Literally!" He flaps and swishes his tail frantically. I see frayed edges. "I have also learned that Anna is one of them! She killed your father!"

What!? Dad was my hero that I always looked up to! How could Anna kill him! Anna was Dad's favorite maid!

"Dracula killed your mother,"he continues, and pouts, unhappily. *Humph.*

"I've always noticed something suspicious or vampire-y about her. And her teeth! She was very—oh no, oh no, oh no no no no no! I've been living with a vampire all my—AAAAHHHHH!!!!!!"

Chapter Six

No Public School. I Don't Wanna Be Called A Homeschool Baby!

"What... are, uhhh, YOU GUYS, doin', umm, uhh, people??" I ask, my hands shaking. I am terrified. My knees feel like rubber. Okay. I am gonna die. Repeat after me. I am gonna die. I am gonna die. My face turns *pale*! I think I'm gonna faint from shock.

What or WHO I see are Dracula and Anna.

Another vampire is carrying a huge,thick blanket to make sure Dracula and Anna don't burn to sooty black ash piles.

"Who ARE you?" I wonder aloud, as Pegasus disappears soundlessly.

"Riley, I'm astonished! I'm Anna, your new mother!" Anna explains, shocked at me.

"New VAMPIRE mother," I mumble under my breath.

"And, this is Drake, my boyfriend," she says, gesturing slowly toward Dracula.

"I am not your boyfriend!!!!" yells Dracula. "I'm zee Chief!!!!

"Chief? Chief of what? Chief Of Bananas?" I ask.

Anna glares at Dracula.

"Anyway, this is my boyfriend!" She smiles fakely.

She glares at Drac. I think he gets it. He shuts up.

"WHAT???!!" I yell. "Dracu—I mean, *Drake* is your new boyfriend?! No offense, but I think, in my opinion, that Drake looks a lot like Dracula the vampire."

Anna and Dracula-oops *Drake* stare at each other in shock. They look shocked and mad at the same time. I wonder if that is called.....shad? I have a habit of joining words, emotions, people, animals, etc., etc.

Before they yell at me, I say, "Never mind."

Humph.

"Okay, Riley. Oh, my! I almost forgot to tell you, Riley! You are finally going to a public school!" Anna says happily as if I'm a torture and making me go there will make her happy.

"What the heck?! A public school! I can't even imagine what that would be like! I've been homeschooled all through second grade till now! I am NOT going to get bullied on a smelly school bus on a freezing day just for public education!! Plus being name called!! They'd call me Rich Girl! Homeschool Baby!! And if the teacher yells at me!

Ohhh, there is *no way* I'm going to put up with that. So, there is NO WAY I'm ever, ever ever going to attend a regular school," I whine, hysterically. "And it's July, so...."

Then I pause, and ask, "Why is there a blanket over your head? It's a million degrees."

Then Anna fumes, "Riley Elizabeth Peterson!! Go to your room NOW!! That'll teach you to mind your own business. Oh, and also, Riley, we are taking your little horse away. FOREVER!!!" She says, proud of her cruel punishment.

She has a sly grin on her face.

"No. This is a joke!" I say, skeptically.

I back away, in the stage of denial. I stop.

I should stand up for myself, I tell myself. *Yeah! Like, who is Anna to take my horse away?! She can't boss me around!* I stand in the face of cruelty. I put my chin up to her. Her face is way more ugly no, hideous, close up than far away. I can see why she puts a lot of makeup on. "But if true, no, you aren't taking *my* Buddy away! He's the only living memory I have of my parents! Besides, he is *way* too tough," I remind her.

Anna looks at Dracula-or Drake. Whatever, I don't care--and nods her head slowly.

"Well, he *is* Pigaseesth, isn't he, masteer?" she mumbles. (*Very* quietly.)

"Yes," replies Drake.

"Okay. If you don't take that consequence, you'll be grounded for a year!" She laughs wickedly, her voice rising again like thunder coming closer in a storm.

"Fine with me!" I say, finishing the huge argument. I storm out of the way to start minding my own business like she said I should.

But I know that Drake is Dracula. Grrrrr..........

•••

We have spaghetti and meatballs with heaps of macaroni and cheese plus heaps of pizza!! Italian food lunch/night! Chef Dana made it. She doesn't know about my parents' death. I just told her that Dad mysteriously went on a job interview for seven months and Mom's boss told her she needs to go to Vienna for something. Or maybe it's... Rome....or Paris. Yep. She's going to Rome, Paris, and Vienna. It's going to be a long time until she gets back. Wait. She's a veterinarian *and* a business woman. That's also why Dad was a billionaire. Well, now *I* am.

Actually, I told everyone that, and only Anna knows how my parents really died. I also tell my enemy the clever lie I made up, I'd rather not tell her name because she is now my sworn enemy for life.

If she reads this book and I tell her name, she is going to scream, throw the book down, and burn it. She's gonna come and find me, and then she's gonna choke me to death.

I'll call her Fancy Pants Ugly Higginbottoms.

Okay.

This will kill her more.

So this is how our friendship became a raging friendship feud.

One day, Fancy Pants Ugly Higginbottoms was prancing around the recess bragging about how her 'glorious' family just won the lottery and our parents are dummies and stupid. (WHICH THEY ARE NOT) Then I told her that was fake and that no parents are dummies or stupid. I told her that money isn't the most important thing in life and that love and family is. She laughed her head off and howled like an orange howler monkey. She told me *I was as dumb as one*. I told the teachers and Fancy Pants Ugly Higginbottoms was in big trouble.

Then the next day, she kicked me square in the face.

"Oh, you did *not!*" I yelled, angrily.

"Well, I just did, you tattletale!" she laughed.

106

The *worst*.

She got expelled for life. No school in the WHOLE planet will take her in. Her parents' don't even know the word 'Homeschool.' That's why she doesn't have *any* education.

I got steamin' mad and told on her parents and told *my* worried parents when they saw the black eye on my face plus my lips were intensely swollen.

Ever since then, I haven't gone to public or private schools anymore, and I am not going *ever*. (Also because the teachers spoke in boring voices and I was getting bored and I was being constantly bullied all the time.)

Then, today, I bump into her with her blood red curling locks and a typical long hot pink dress with red overalls that barely fit her (I bet it's for three year old kids), and she says, "Look who's here! Dummy RiRi wanna cwy to your mommy and daddy with your lame gwey sweatshiwt?" she taunts, adding, "Hah! That's the clothes you bought? I thought you were rich!"

I fume and grind my teeth in anger and sigh. "Look, I know who I am and you don't mess with it. We've all grown out of your silly taunting lectures and we're almost out of middle school, so either grow up, or lose your friends. Well, if you have any," I tell her.

She harrumphs in shock and crosses her arms. "Well! Look who's—" I shove her out of the way.

"I don't wanna hear it," I add.

"Where *are* your dummy parents anyway?" she asks, in her regular snobby and even more annoying tone. I turn from confident to defiant.

"My dad is doing a job interview in Greece and my mom is on a work trip to Paris," I tell her, quickly and rapidly.

"Oh. Whatevs. Nothing I can bug you about," says Fancy Pants Ugly Higginbottoms, uninterested. She walks away. "Except your stupid dog!" She snorts.

I roll my eyes. General Puppy barks loudly at the insult. FPUHB (Fancy Pants Ugly Higginbottoms) flinches.

I would've said, *"Nobody calls my dog stupid!"* and yank her girly overalls and spit on her face, but I decide to prove I'm more mature than her and just say, "Ugh. What an arrogant little girl." She is so-o nasty.

"Bye, Fancy Pants Ugly Higginbottoms!" I yell. (I am just covering her real name. I actually said her real name. Not Fancy Pants Ugly Higginbottoms. That means if I do say it, she would be my worst archenemy, even worse than we are now. And she would go bonkers! Then we would kill each other! Literally! I can already see the blood...)

We walk in separate directions, each like we have sibling rivalry. We have a *friend* rivalry. No. An *enemy* rivalry.

Anyway, FPUHB hates books, so she's not gonna read this book. I'll tell her name. It is Prudence Grossman. She's a sourpuss.

I go to the colossal gym. Not any fitness or anything kind of gym, a *gymnastics* gym. I *love* gymnastics. It's awesome! I won't call it a gymnasium. Why?

Because gymnos, the root word of gymnasium means 'naked' in Greek.

Yes. Gymnasium means 'the naked room.' (They do sports naked.) In Greek.

I go to the locker room. (Yes! A locker room!) Bella and I share the locker room. There are two lockers, plus two shower thingies if we need that after a day of soccer and gymnastics. Has doors.

I change into my leotard. It is the kind that gymnasts use in the Olympics. The leotard has a sleek black horse silhouette that is rearing up; It has a blue and purple background with ice twinkles.

I then step lightly as a feather onto the mat. I sneak a little smile and then I run faster than the wind. I push off the vault with a *THUMP!* I spin one-two-three times and do a triple somersault in the air before landing on the ground and holding my arms up. I whoop with pure joy. My arms fling up in the air to make a *woosh!* I bow.

"Ri! Good one!" a familiar voice cheers. Bella pounds her fist into the air. I pause. I look at Bella. I run over to her. I smile.

"Thank you, thank you." I smirk, imitating a famous person.

Bel smiles. She shrugs. "I'll change my shirt into *my* leotard." She jogs gingerly over to the locker room. In ten seconds, she's back in the leotard that has a German Shepherd silhouette that is leaping swiftly. It has a fire background...with skeleton trees. They look like they were in a terrible wildfire. Bel is the fierce and humble kind of person.

I smile. She grins too. Then I jog over to the uneven bars. Bella pads over to the high balance beam. I stand on the bars.

I leap expertly over the bars onto the higher one. I swing back and forth. Back and forth. Back and forth. I flip into a handstand on the bar.

I flip over again and again. I swing down and up again. I flip two times and leap effortlessly onto the lower bar.

I swing up and down, doing handstands and epic twists. I flip onto the higher bar once again. The bar creaks. I do several handstands and flips before twisting three times. I soar like a free bird. I land with a thump and hold up my hands.

I glance at Bella, doing flips and cartwheels and aerials on the narrow beam. I grin. I go over to do floor practice. I run and push off and leap into the air. I flip and tumble, twisting five times, doing arches and back handsprings over and over again. I twirl my wrists. I cross my legs, I pause, and then I continue. I flip. I am a blur of black hair, purple and blue, legs and hands. I jump into a straight split. One of the hardest ones I have ever done. It is *perfect!* I point my toes. I jump up and do my long floor routine.

Bella, on the other hand, is on the high uneven bars. She is flipping and doing handstands. I go to the beam. I get onto it, and I steady myself.

'I got this. Pegsy, wish me luck.'

I point my toes, raise my arms, and flip into an aerial. I wobble. Eesh. Not the best sign if you wanna be a future Olympian athlete.

I hold up my hands, and do a backflip.

"Nice!" says Bella.

I smile. I split into a split. Duh!

Then I do a series of flips, and handstands on the balance beam, which is four inches wide! Then, I do a backflip, followed by flips to dismount perfectly.

Bella went home now. I run over to my dozing Buddy. I wake the drowsy horse and take him to the woods near our home so that no one can see him. I turn him into Pegsy.

"Whaaaaaat doooo you waaaaant?" Pegs groans, half asleep. He yawns again. "I was happily sleeping, until *someone* woke me up."

"Pegs. Look. Anna is not good and she is *horrible*. You saw Dracula. You are gonna have to be safe. You will be

Pegsy only in this dense woodland. So that the Vamps won't be able to find you. But only at night. Kay?" I warn him.

"Okay. Did you just wake me to advise me? You woke me up for this? Wow, how annoying! How rude! Y-you may have done that in the daytime....." He trails off. I snap so he can suddenly remember what I said just a second ago. His head shoots up like a cannon. His eyes pop widely.

"Oh yes. And anyway, turning me into the, um... quite muscular stallion at night will let the vampires find us *quicker*. We must not do it at night. We must do it in the daytime, where the sun is bright and shining. That way, they won't find us. In the daylight, I hide from vampire sight. Plus, any vampire would ignite and turn into ashes in daylight." Pegsy explains patiently like a calm teacher with misbehaving students.

I bite my lip. "I guess you are right..." I trail off.

"Well, about me being handsome and muscular or the other thing. You know, I am quite the pretty fellow," he brags.

I roll my eyes.

I see that Pegsy is glowing brightly like a beacon or a flare.

Hmmm..... he is right.......the vampires could find him any moment right now if I don't turn him into Buddy.

Whoosh!

I look up to see what made the swift whooshing noise. I first think maybe it's an owl, or a bird, but no!

A vampire. No. No! NO!

"No. No no no no no!" I whisper softly. In an invisible flash, I surely guess, Pegsy disappears mysteriously.

Phew! But wait. The vampire.Where is he?Or maybe *she?* I glance up.

Where is the vampire? I look around.

There.

There. Is. The. Vampire!

There, in the woods is a pale, long haired woman. She has absolute pure raven-black hair that is waist long, thoroughly brushed and shiny. I can tell she is a vampire because she has long, dagger-like teeth and an atrocious overbite.

Longer that *Anna's.*

You don't need to see how long Anna's is. They stick outta her mouth. Well only the top two ones. Not the bottom ones.

That would be weird.

114

If Anna's looks like a tiger's, this woman's looks like a saber-toothed-cat's.

Yup.

"H-hello" I stammer in fear. "I-I just got lost. Please. L-leave m-me alone. P-p-please." I almost drop to a whisper.

"Okay?????" the mysterious woman says, confused face. She looks shocked that such a young child would stand up to such a horrible stranger. Her voice is sharp and low. She sounds like a strict college professor.

I narrow my eyes. I recognize this woman...
She is the woman who chased me into the dense forest the day my parents died. Is wearing *the Victorian dress.*

"Aren't you the woman who chased me and carelessly killed my parents?" I mention, agitated. "A-aren't you gonna hurt me? Viciously bite me with your vampire t-teeth?" I squeak.

Her face turns practically into a strawberry. "*Vhat* deed you ssaaaaaay?" she asks, narrowing her eyes too, with a strong, *spooky* Transylvanian accent.

She now sounds more vampire-ish.

"I-I'm gonna leave now," I whimper, frightened. I wish I didn't say the part about the vampire stuff. I wish I had just gone and been home.

I wish.

She grabs me by the collar. "Oh, *you're* not going anywhere!" laughs the woman.

Her voice sounds like a craggy witch. Her cold, bony, fine, long fingered hand knocks the breath outta me.

I get hit with bricks with a spectacular idea.

I roll my eyes to the side, playing dead.

I pretend to lay limp like a dead rabbit in the jaws of a hunting dog.

Perhaps a Beagle or an Irish Wolfhound.

It works!

The vampire thinks that I choked to death and drops me like a rag doll.

Ouch!

She then utters something that sounds like a curse. It sends creeps through my sensitive, bony spine.

"Now vhere eez that vrretched stallion ov Olymups that gould bring uz vampires to Olymups? I have thoo vind heem. Jeef has sent me on an impordant meessson. Eev I vail, I vould be having zee zurn. And I vould be redooced thoo ashees." She shakes her hairy head. Her hair swishes like a horse's tail swishing away annoying flies.

I shudder. Then, I get an amazing idea!

Maybe, maybe, I could dress like a vampire, and talk like one, look like one, and pretend to be one. Then at the vampire palace, I could learn the secrets. Like all the stuff in the palace. That way, I, Riley E. Peterson, would learn the secrets of the vampire race.

I wait until the murderous woman is far from sight.

Then, slowly and carefully, I rise from the dirt-ish and grassy floor.

I hide behind a swaying, greenish moss covered tree. I summon forth Pegsy.

"Pegasus. Please. Give me the power to walk quietly. Not making a sound. Please?" I ask him when he appears.

He nods.

'Wait. Let me ponder quickly about what the spell is.' He sends me a message through my mind and mumbles something in Olympian.

I try walking noisily.

No sound!!

'Yay!' I think silently like a mouse.

'And will you make me look like a vampire and have a Transylvanian accent, so that I will blend into them and so that I will know their plans? After that, will you turn me

back to Riley? Please, with carrots and ambrosia?' I send a message back to his mind.

Pegsy shakes his head. **'As I cannot turn people or any living being into any other form, except I. That will not work. As that is also dangerous. I, or all of Olympus cannot bear the loss of such an important child. No. And the foolish vampires will easily pick you out as they shall see you not being able to suck blood like how they do. Dracula shall figure it out soon. No, child.'** He sends a message.

Okay.

"At least let me follow her!" I hiss quietly, careful not to let the murderous woman hear an audible sound.

Pegsy disappears. I guess that's a yes???

Aaand so I follow her.

I dash quickly, just two trees behind her.

I hear her muttering and shaking her head. "Jeef is gonna be berry mad at me."

I follow her, eavesdropping, as I observe like a vulture. She is blabbering and shaking her head like a very wet, drippy dog. "I have to find that foul mad-horse. He is important. He will take us to Olymups vhen vee veed him the stinky, smelly zubzdance that vill put him under our control. Mwah haha!!!!!!!!!!!!"

I freeze like a statue.

Liquid that puts Pegsy under complete control of the malevolent vampires?

Not on *my* watch.

I grind my teeth.

If I were a fiery dragon, smoke would've risen from my narrow nostrils. I would've been so mad, I would've burned that Victorian-dressed-vampire to ashes in a blinking second.

I run like lightning and I take out my flashlight I always carry with me in my jeans shorts. (I have a lot of jeans.) I flip it on and point the beam towards the woman. I've had enough. In a puff of smoke, the woman disappears, before vowing a curse in a fading voice, filled with agony. "I vill have revenge! YOU SHALL SUFFER........"

Chapter Seven

Through Pegasus's crystal ball.

"I had no idea you had a crystal ball!" I exclaim, hypnotized, while looking into the shimmering glass. Yesterday's event was way too traumatic, and I've been wondering.

Wondering.

What had the vampire said? What was the second curse? The woman had said, "I vill have revenge. YOU SHALL SUFFER....."

What did that mean?

I don't know. It's been keeping me worried all day!

Never mind! What's in the crystal ball?

"You zed eet vould vurk, Anna. You vailed," Dracula says sternly. *"I am deezabointed."*

"But jeef!! How gould I know zat zee leetle guhl could vee zo glever?" Anna protests.

Dracula's clean shining, polished black boots click and clack on the smooth, hard marble floor. He grumbles in

frustration and rubs his temples madly. "How could you
doo thees? Pigaseesth got avay."

"But I had to! I could not let Riley know vee are
vampires!" Anna yells furiously.

"You are not alloved to zyell ath me! do you vant to
have a zurn?" Dracula says wickedly as a grin slides slowly
across his face. The 'zurn' meant that Anna had to be rudely
hauled out in the blistering hot sun and burned to black
ashes.

"No!!! I doo not vant a zurn! Blease! No zurn! No
zurn," Anna cries hysterically.

I gasp. I can't believe it! Dracula would really do that!
Pegasus looks at me in horror. I realize he means that they
want to get rid of him.

"Pegasus, can you believe that! He wants to get rid of
you! And Anna! I don't even hear her saying words like vant
or something."   He nods. Tears, I think, escape his hazel
eyes.

"Riley. I do not want to ever, ever leave you. You chose
me at the stables. No one else did. They just blew raspberries
at me. No one has been so kind to me. The farmer... well he

kicked me and spit right on me. I kicked him back, FYI. Promise me, never to ever leave me. In your life."

"I promise. But why are you saying this stuff? It's not like you are dying. Wait! ARE YOU?????"

"No. But I just want to tell you that. Plus, I'm immortal. You should be feeding me sweet stuff. Cereal that is made of pure sugar. Or sugar. Or HONEY!!!! Or even all of them combined!!!!!!!!!!!"

I never saw Pegasus so happy. "Pegasus, can I call you..... Pegsy?"

"Sure," he says.

I look at the crystal clear ball.

"Count! gome eere drright now! Dake Anna. Give ver zee zurn," Dracula says, his face toward the balcony, and his cape billowing in the night breeze. "Vonze zis traitor, Anna iz gone, ve vill launch vull addack. Diley's 'ouse eez not var avay from 58th sthreeth, za blace vhere our gastle eez." He cackles wickedly.

"Eet iz night dime. Jood I throw er een za zlammer?" the count asks nervously.

"Yezz! Vool! You chicken? Throw zer there!" Dracula roars. "YOU BRAINLESS!" His spittle sprays everywhere.

Anna, however, remains silent. She lays limp in the count's arms.

"The invisible gas in the injection I threw on her vill make unconscious for five days. Tomorrow, she's dead as a doorknob," Dracula sneers madly.

Dracula! How come he's soo single-minded? "Have some feeling mister!" I say. I bet his heart is ice. Pegasus has no feeling on his face.

"Anna does deserve it. She wants to kill me and you," Pegasus says.

I remember in realization what Dracula said. "Pegsy! Dracula! He's gonna attack us tomorrow! He says the vampire castle is on 58th street! We must be prepared for tomorrow's attack! We could start working up traps. One of them is that we could dig a hole, fill it with garlic, let them fall in, and they will burn to ashes! We could put crosses and they would crumble to dust. How's that Pegsy?" I ask.

"Absolutely!" says Pegsy, beaming. "We will get rid of them all."

Ha! Pegasus and I have the absolute best ideas! "*We will get rid of them all.*" He's the cutest horse when he's formal. Me spending more time with Pegasus has really improved my exciting life. He really gets it. He really gets *me*.

That's why I love him.

Well, as family, not a crush.

No way. I don't think I'll ever meet a handsome, cute boy like in the magazines teen girls my age moon over.

Ugh.

I pity them and their pathetic, gross lives.

<Yawn...>

Anyway, yep. Pegsy is my BFF, and nobody—even vampires— will ever get rid of him.

Not on my watch.

He knows I love him, and he especially cares for me, too. We're great people and a great team.

Chapter Eight

Little Foal

After I eat dinner, I play video games while I digest. I plan on doing more gymnastics later.

After about an hour, I go downstairs, pass two grand halls, four doors, five corridors, and finally, the gymnastics room. I bet I did all the exercise already! Jeez, did my parents spend *all* their money on this huge mansion? Anyway, as I walk into the gigantic gym, I hear footsteps echoing on the marble floor. They start out slow, then faster, then super fast, then they slow down.

<Tip-tap...tip-tap...tip-tap-tip-tap-tip-tap-ti-ta-ti-ta-tap...tap...tap...>"Hello?" I ask, nervously, "Are you in there?" *<Tip-tap>* I move forward. A shadow appears. It seems to be balancing on its hands. My palms become clammy. "Who are you?" I stammer. "Huh?" it asks. "Who said that?" It looks like it's threatening to hurt me with its

fists. The voice is familiar. It sounds like a girl. I tiptoe closer to her until I get a full image.

Deep strawberry blonde hair? Check.

Intense freckles? Check.

Long legs? Check.

Bella? What is she doing here? "Bel? Did you text me that you were going to be here?" Her face turns red. "Ummmmm...." she stammers. She takes her phone out of her bag and types something. My phone dings. I take it out of my pocket and read my message.

I'm going 2 ur house 2 do gymnastics.

I roll my eyes. "Now I did." I stifle a small laugh. "It's okay if you didn't tell me," I say. I go into my stall and put my leotard on.

I start warming up. Walking on your hands. Straddle, Pike, Arch, jogging, head rolls, splits. Side split and middle split. Ouch! The middle split HURTS. I do a back handspring.

Bel claps her hands. She's an awesome bestie if you're seeking permanent moral support. "Hey, can you do a back handspring?" I ask.

Bella doesn't know how to do a back handspring.

She can do an Ariel.

After gymnastics and a shower, (a shower helps when you sure are sweaty!) I go to bed.

When I wake up in the morning, I curl up with an awesome book.

The book I'm reading is called <u>Little Foal And The People.</u> It's pretty good.

The young horse reared. She didn't want to become meat. The men had food shortages in the blistering, make-your-nose-fall-off cold.

They each, one by one, butchered each one of their horses.

Poor guys.

So faithful to their masters, but to die in misery, all to be eaten by their dishonest masters. Now there were a handful of horses, the beasts now so thin and lean, struggling to survive, knowing they wouldn't.

They would die.

The intimidating foal stampeded until she stopped in her tracks to find her mother and father being walked to doom.

While she was racing across the field, one minute her parents were there, now they were gone.

She whinnied in fright and confusion. She raced everywhere. They must have become meat, now, too.

She plopped down heavily napping with all her older brothers and sisters who had thankfully survived.

They had run away, to a very secret place, starting to sprout with lush grass.

These relaxing breaks always made her cool down after she lost a fellow loved one.

This happened to her a lot, and even though she was the youngest in her family, she knew it would happen to her anytime soon.

Why, she was too rebellious for anyone to let her down easy and be fed to the butchers last.

All of her living relatives were young, and not ready to eat yet.

As much pain she felt knowing she would die like her parents some day, she knew it was coming and she was prepared.

Of course you would think a horse doesn't know how to escape, but she was a smart young horse and she had a plan.

She was wise, wise as a raven.

She had the instincts of the wild ones.

Brave as a warrior.

Then, suddenly, she heard a rustle.

A howl.

The tiny youngster's eyes fluttered open.

Wolves!

She neighed sharply, alarmed. Maybe she wouldn't die the same as her mom and dad. Maybe the wolves would attack. The pack of starving hunters ran while howling their unwelcoming song.

The foal stared into the bush. She ran to it and hid behind it.

She decided to doze off in this healthy green bush.

But she couldn't sleep.

The frightening wolves were howling too loud and she knew that they were out to get her.

She warned her siblings with a panicked whinny. The wolves heard her gentle caution and smelled her grungy body.

She put her brown nose into the leafy bush, afraid. What was she to do? She was only a small horse! Hope was all lost... except for one hairy canid who seemed to be quite interested in this clever little filly.

Yellow glinting eyes greeted her.

And a growl.

She looked at this young wolf -who actually looked a bit like a cub-and pinned her hoof down. She was locked in his eyes. Nope. She had to protect her family! She shook her head.

She jumped back and fled.

The foal ran faster than the wind, her long, clumsy legs spindling faster.

She bashed painfully into a tree. She shook herself, and ran faster than a jet quicker than ever before.

She ducked behind some brambles and heard familliar voices.

"Where's the foal? She is next for butchering. She will make us starve if we don't kill 'er right now. I want 'er to be right in front of my polished boots."

The man paused, hearing what made the hoof beats.

Then, he saw the foal.

Oh no.

This klutzy little foal was about to be dinner.

She ran faster.

The man ran even faster.

But she was too petrified for this man to catch up with her.

He would scoop her up and say, "You're about to be eaten, little one!" He would roar with laughter, looking at her thrashing in fear.

She was too pained to let that happen to her and her family.

She sent a quiet signal for her brother to come closer.

She didn't need to tell her sisters. They were already faithfully by her skinny side.

A fact about her is that she was not only the fastest and sneakiest of the group, but she was also the skinniest. She was so thin you could see her tense ribs.

She ran faster, fearing that she wouldn't even be able to run anymore. It was hard for her to breathe, too. She was panting. Panting hard.

With the man behind her, the wolves chasing her, the youngster ran faster than Secretariat, the famous racehorse. (That was going to happen a lot of years later. Secretariat was going to be a star centuries later.)

Suddenly, a sheer cliff came in front of the herd of horses.

Without thinking, they thundered on and leaped like a snow leopard.

The foal thought that she was an eagle, like the ones she saw in her homeland.

Free.

She loved feeling like flying. Much better than the feeling of being cooped up in a butcher's land.

All too soon, they thudded onto the other side of the snow-covered canyon. Her brother, a colt, skidded to the canyon ridge. The foal was covered head to toe on her brown body with icy, soft snow.

Brrrr... It was freezing!

She had never felt snow in her life. Her yearling sisters had. She was born in the springtime in that year, so she had never encountered glistening, white snow. She had no idea how cold it could get.

Yet, she'd never witnessed something so beautiful.

It was fascinating. Alluring!

She played in the snowdrift with her brother for hours.

This blizzard was incredibly new to her, and it should take weeks to get used to, but at least she wouldn't be able to get fed up with the rude butchers.

She settled down.

Snow was like a bed. A bed she could get anytime here.

At last, they, the herd of young horses, were safe.

They were home.

I love this book. I know this doesn't have The Men that much, but it is their horse. I can also really relate to the young foal. She was also endangered by scary people. Her parents died because of these monsters. She had to plan. She had to think! She was really brave for her age. I don't think I can relate to that last part, though. I'm not too brave.

Ding Dong!

I jump. Who rang the doorbell? It absolutely can't be Fancy Pants Ugly Higginbottoms. No way.

I rush downstairs, racing down the steps two at a time.

It is Bella and Steph. In black clothes each.

Chapter Nine

Mmmmmm...Lemonade, Steph!

They've been at a funeral.

"Oh," I exclaim softly. "I'm so sorry!

I welcome them inside.

They sorrowfully step in, after brushing their dusty shoes on the welcome mat. Bella is weeping heavily (and quietly). Tears gush out of her eyes. "I miss her," she manages to sob out as I hug them both.

Bella's sister is now close to crying. Tears spill out of Stephanie's green eyes like a waterfall. I hand her a tissue. She dabs her eyes then blows her nose. "I miss her, too, I guess."

Bella rolls her eyes.

"Who died?" I ask carefully and quietly, letting them mourn.

"M-mom. She—she died," Stephanie croaks out.

"What?! Ms. Hamilton is so nice!" I almost shout in fear.

I think this has something to do with the wicked, single minded vam-poop-ires!

"Oooh! Whoever did this to my best friend and *her sister* is gonna have to pay," I say, in a tough voice.

"No, Riley. We don't even know who did it! She was murdered in her bed. We just know it was a group of people wearing dark capes for the men, and long black dresses for the women. They all were wearing sunglasses and black face masks over their mouths. Well, at one point, they did take off their masks, and then they were wearing fake vampire teeth. It was really weird to watch. We tried to save her, but then this one woman bit my mom with her stupid fake teeth." Bella pouted. "Then, Mom died."

I don't think those are fake... I assume in my mind. I don't say it out loud, because she might think I'm a weirdo and leave.

I just say, "Sounds scary. It's over now, though. Your dad is probably coming here from Canada to take care of you." I hold her hand.

"No. I told dad, and he said no. He said he isn't coming back," Bella says, her voice choking.

I look down, feeling bad for her. I would feel horrible if my parents were separated, my mom died, and my dad in Canada wouldn't come back for me!

"Oh," I only say.

We sit there in silence for just a moment. Just alone with our bottomless thoughts.

I finally change the subject.

"Do you want some lemonade?" I ask, standing up.

"Sure," Bella tells me.

"No, thanks," Stephanie says.

Bella rolls her eyes. "Ugh. Steph's trying to avoid all sugar-y things. She calls it her 'early diet'." She scoffs, "But surely, you couldn't resist drinking this... Delicious, refreshing, cooling, mouth-watering..." Bella takes a great big slurp of the lemonade I just handed her, "...Aaaaahhh...beverage? Mmmmm...Lemonade, Steph!" She licks her lips continuously.

She's being so hard on Stephanie, Stephanie's literally sweating!

"Um, I don't even mind! That... <gulp> so called 'succulent' drink! Heh heh!" I could tell she did mind. She was licking her lips and her stomach was growling (no, *rumbling*) REALLY loudly.

"It's no problem, Bel. Stephanie can have her 'early diet'." I tell Bella, making air quotation marks for 'early diet.' I secretly make a cuckoo sign.

But, does she listen?

No.

"Okay, B, I think you made your point." Stephanie is on the brink of surrendering, when I tell Bel, "Bella? Can you listen to me? Please? You almost never do that." I feel kind of uncomfortable saying this to Bella. She takes things so seriously.

She might want to fight.

Or maybe she just won't listen to me. But, she does.

"Riley? Did you say I don't listen?" she asks. I nod my head carefully.

"I listen! Ri, I don't wanna make this a thing, but I actually do listen," she admits. The other thing is that she almost never wants to make it a 'thing.'

Except she always does.

"Okay. Yeah, it's just, sometimes you don't listen to me. Like, once in a while. But usually when you need to do something really important," I say, proving that I really want to still be friends forever.

Bella shrugs. "Sounds like me," she agrees.

137

Then, we must've all remembered why Bel and Stephanie were here at the same time, because then we all look sad again.

"Chin up, guys! You'll figure this out. I know it. Stephanie, do you do gymnastics?" I ask, as Bella looks grateful I changed the subject.

"Yes," Stephanie says. "I used to, but I started track."

Bella gets the idea.

"Well, I sure do! Let's do it. Wait, actually I forgot my leotard," Bella says, kind of disappointed.

"Not to worry. We got backups in the gym," I say.

Chapter Ten

Gymnastics With The Hamiltons

"Wait. No. Way. You have a gymnasium?!" Stephanie asks.

I hate calling it a gymnasium. It means 'the naked place' in Greek. Gross. The ancient Greeks did exercise nude.

"Of course!" I say, ignoring the fact that she said 'Gymnasium.' "Here, I'll show you." I walk them down to the rooms, corridors, steps, until we get there.

"Gee, I wish I were as rich as you!" Stephanie whines.

"It's not as good as you think. Everybody thinks I'm a stuck-up snob like the cliches. I'm really not!" I sigh, "Plus, I have the worst maid!" I yell, particularly talking about Anna.

I know she is in Drake's prison. Dracula's, really. When Anna used to go out, to go to the vampire palace, I didn't know. When she introduced me to Drake, I thought she was going out for dates, but now I know it was for vampire meetings.

"I'm gonna go get my leotard," Bella says.

"Me too," Stephanie says.

"Wait. I need to know your size, Stephanie," I tell her.

"What do you mean?" she asks.

"Like, your leotard size," I explain. Then she tells me. XL.

I find her a turquoise leotard with light pink cherry blossom petal pictures scattered on it. Bella finds the exact same copy of her usual leotard in her size. I put my leotard on, and cartwheel around the room. I do some deep pondering about the death of the Hamilton sisters' mother.

Why would the vampires hurt Ms. Hamilton? They don't have a magic animal! But what if they do? What if Bella has to do with this? I don't get it! They have garlic and other Italian stuff all the time! The vampires would die!

I do a round off to jump on a balance beam. I practice on balance beams a lot.

What? Don't judge me. I wanna be an Olympic competitor. I'll do gymnastics.

I'll win in the Top Five.

First place, Riley Elizabeth Peterson!

I do aerials.

Then, I do a forward handspring afterwards to get off.

I do a headstand and hold it for a while. *Do they have one and not have told me about it?* I think to myself.

140

I'm still holding it and it really hurts. I get pretty dizzy. Bella's one level lower than me. She's level 9. She hasn't been practicing as long as me. Stephanie's a level lower.

I do a back tuck on the floor.

When they leave, we all have sad looks on our faces. Their mom died. I can't forget that.

"Riley! You have a viola lesson," one of my still-here-maids comes into the grand hall.

It used to be my dad who said that.

"Okay!" I run upstairs into my room.

Chapter Eleven

My new song.

When I'm there, I grab my viola case and take my instrument out. Then the bow. I run outta the room. Out!

Careful!

It almost teeters but I balance it. I run into the music room.

Wow.

My parents have such a big house! Sometimes, I get lost in the halls! My dad is a—was a— billionaire, and I inherited all his money.

Woop-woop!

Who's a rich girl? Imma rich girl!

But, uh, y'all know, I won't spend all my money onna shoppin' spree at the mall... heh heh...

Yeah, I'm *deeeefinitely* gonna donate all the money to charity.

What?!

I *am!!!!!*

Okay. I'm gonna do a little charity.

Anyway, the viola teacher, Karen, comes into the room. "Hello, Riley! Always nice to see you," Karen greets me. Her British accent is twangy. And a bit uneasy.

She's always so polite to people. If she'd let everyone go ahead at the supermarket checkout counter (she does) she'd be there forever! (she usually is there for a *long* time.)

"You too." I smile.

"Thank you. Well, continuing on to our last session, last week really, we were practicing the D string, correct?" she asks me.

"Correct. In fact, I started practicing 'Ode To Joy'! It didn't sound very good, though." I admit.

"Well, you know what they say! Practice makes man perfect! Anyway, could I hear your D string?" she asks.

Ugh! Does she have to say *MAN*!?! That's sexist.

"Sure," I say. I play the D string very carefully.

She claps her hands.

"Brilliant! I love it! How about I hear your 'Ode To Joy', since your D string's so perfect?" she asks, politely. Her strawberry blonde hair, with bits of creamy blonde, waves like ripples.

"Well, I guess. Okay." It sounds kind of annoying and when I hit this one note, it sounds like a frog with a sore throat. General Puppy howls miserably when he hears my horrendous screech. He comes running into the music room and when he sees Karen, he sniffs her hand. I giggle.

"Still needs more practice. But that's still great! Have you made up any songs yet?" she asks. General Puppy starts licking my viola. "Ew! General Puppy! Stop it!" I bark.

"Riley? Have you made up any songs yet?" Karen repeats. I look back at her, wiping my viola. "Oh!" I nod. "With all the strings I know how to do," I say.

"Please show me. I must know how it goes!" Karen says with coaching and curiosity.

I sigh.

It's still a work in progress.

I think about Buddy.

Then, I play the most beautiful G string in my head.

Now all I have to do is to play it in real life. Then, I do it. Then, another note. Then, another G. And then a buncha different notes.

Another note. Then, I play it from the heart. I move my viola in concentration, not doing it slowly. My bow dances on the instrument. I move my bow across all the strings to make exquisite sounds.

When I'm done, I hold the note I finish with. Then, with a sudden stop, I take the bow quickly off the viola's strings.

Karen just stares at me. Then, she slowly claps. She's very dramatic. "Wonderful, Riley! How did you do that?" she asks me.

"I don't know," I shrug. "I just thought of it."

Chapter Twelve

"Bella, we Should Dress up as grown-ups, get a beard, board a plane and go after Steph,"

After viola practice, I write in my diary some more. I'm not gonna show you cause diarrhea—NO!!! (Hahaha) I mean *diaries* are secret. Too much privacy. Especially mine.

Fine. I'll tell ya what I wrote.

Well......only like a summary though.

I had viola practice. An awesome lesson I learned today.

I did other stuff. I also played a long game of soccer with Bella. I got new soccer cleats from my allowance. Plus Anna left her wallet behind when going to Dracula's. So I have her wallet and my allowance money. It's not like stealing, like how a thief does. Anna's probably dead and I'm an orphan. For years! Well not twelve months, but still a long time.

I mean, you get it... right? I'm just a poor little orphan. A thirteen-year-old girl who's been forced to follow annoying rules her maid made up and is sick and tired of them.

What? Don't judge me.

I did not use a single penny from the wallet. Although I did check how much money there was. And, jeez, is that woman greedy! Yeesh!

$10,000?!?! And that too monthly!?!?!?!? She has so much! AND just before my parents died, she asked them for higher pay! What a terrible, greedy hog I had, bossing me around in my house! I'm almost *glad* she died!

Then again, Poor Anna!

Dead.

Dead.

Dead.

But, on the other hand, she *did* help work with Dracula to kill my parents...

"Ri! Ri! Ri," Bella calls.

I jerk my head.

Bel is running to my house.

She opens the door wide.

Quickly, I hide the black, batty wallet in the oak table drawer. It does have bat pictures.

Weird.

"Oh ... hi!" I chuckle nervously.

"Ri! It's an emergency! An absolute must go now emergency!" Bella pants, her sweaty hands on her jeans, wheezing. She can barely breathe at all. She can't say another word. I mildly assumed it was one of her 'fake emergencies' where Bella thinks it's something serious, but it's just something like, 'We ran out of toilet paper.' But, I was still concerned. "What is it!?" I practically shout like an orange howler monkey. Then she utters three, terrible words.

"Stephanie. Ran. Away."

I gasp.

I should've seen this coming! She's a teenager and the last thing she needs is for her parents to divorce and her mom dead!

"Bel! For realsies, though?!"

She nods her head quickly and vigorously. "I checked the WHOLE house. The trash cans, the attic, the boilers; She's not there."

"We gotta do something," she protests.

"And fast." I say, jumping up and ready to go.

Bella runs out of the house and motions for me to follow her.

148

I slip my white sneakers with no laces on and race out the door. (I pick the shoes fastest to get on, but also easy to run in. My sneakers are slip-on sneakers.)

Bel and I run like the wind, the gentle breeze now whipping in our long hair. It is a good thing it's sunny out. Bella isn't her chatty self anymore. She's not optimistic or positive. She's as serious as an owl. Like Minerva/Athena! Wait. How do I know? Right. Latin Class. Or my math tutor! He doesn't move a muscle. Seriously, Bella can be serious, but she's my awesome friend and I won't let her stay that way forever! "Bella! Cheer up, girl! We're going to find her." I motivate her.

She smiles at me. "I'm gonna be okay, Ri. It's just that... She's my sister. One time, I ran away, too. But she found me. Plus, she didn't take the garbage out. And it's her turn! The garbage stinks. I can't throw anything away before fainting and dying from the fumes." Bella complains. "She can't just run off on me like that. Not how my dad did."

Bel clutches her side. She flops down on the park bench.

"My stomach hurts." She clamps her palm on her side. "I think I ran too much." She groans painfully.

"You rest. Walk. We'll look for her. Are you okay?" I pat her back.

I look down at my shoes and sigh.

But, then, I get an idea of where Stephanie might be!

"That's it!" I squeal, proudly.

Bella looks up at me, confused. "What's 'It'?" she asks.

"Well! When you said 'Not how my dad did', I got an idea! Your dad lives in Canada, right?" I ask.

Bella shakes her head. "Woah, Riley! You don't mean—"

I nod, a smirk on my face.

"No! We can't walk from Austin, Texas to Nova Scotia, Canada!" she finishes, confusion crossing her eyes.

"No, Bel! Think! How would you go to Nova Scotia? Using a plane!"

She smiles. "I miss my dad, but I don't wanna go to Canada!" she exclaims.

"Do you wanna find your sister?" I ask.

"Well, yeah, but..."

"You know you want to go," I reassure Bella. She nods.

"Uh-huh!" I whoop. I've always wanted to go to Canada. "When did you last see Steph?" I ask like a detective.

150

"Two days ago. She said she was going on a two day sleepover with her friends. But when she didn't come home today, I called her friends, but they said there was no sleepover. Then I suspected that she had run—or drove—away," she rushes.

"Does Steph have a driving license and a car?" I ask.

Bel nods. "A yellow Tesla. We aren't *all* poor. We're rich too."

Yep. Steph has the coolest Tesla ever! It's yellow, and has these seats that make whatever sound you want when you sit on it.

Aaaaanyway, "Aha! Steph must've driven over to the international airport wherever it is! Bel, did Steph leave with Ms. Hamilton's wallet and stuff?" I ask.

"Y-yeah!" says Bella, starting to understand Steph's unraveling plan. It was like ... a jigsaw puzzle. One important detail followed by another important part, finally solving the puzzle.

"That means, over the past two days, Steph has been driving over to the huge airport to fly in a plane, to get to Nova Scotia, Canada!" Bel and I hypothesize in unison, jumping to the final conclusion.

"JINX!"

"Knock on wood!"

"I don't think we can be able to go and get Steph. We're kids! Not adults! The flight attendants or anyone else on the plane or airport won't let us go! They'd say, 'Whoa! Kids don't go on plane flights alone! You are not allowed!' And then laugh! 'Hahaha.' And I don't think *we* can go!" Bella is bursting into tears! She wipes her eyes from the back of her hand.

I drop my smile. "Yeah." Even if I could, I couldn't leave Buddy and General Puppy alone, either!

Now Bella is more lonely than ever!

"We can't drive cars... We can't even *walk* to the airport! It's too far away! We're doomed. Face it." She sighs.

But then, both of our faces light up! We must've been thinking the same thing at that same moment!

"Are you thinking what I'm thinking?!" I ask her, "If you're thinking we can call Stephanie, then yes!" Bella cries. I can't believe we didn't think of that!"

Bella dials her number. (908)-123-456.

Ha! 123-456! What a funny number.

"Hey, Steph? Yeah, this is she... Yeah? Oh. Sorry to bother you... Y-yeah, I'll hang up." Bella presses the red button on her phone meaning that she wants to hang up.

She places it in her pocket.

"So?" I ask, "How'd it go?" She shakes her head.

"Stephanie wasn't there. It was just her boyfriend, Noah." She sighs.

"How do you know it's her boyfriend?" I ask her, kind of gagging.

"He said so," she replied.

"Well, do you even know where your sister *is*?" I say.

Bella nods. "Noah said that she was in Nova Scotia, and she forgot her phone in New York City. She's driving back."

My eyes widened.

New York City!

Why would Steph go east to New York City, leave her phone there, and drive away?

Anyway, "New York? I would *love* to go there!" I shout, with passion. I've been there before, though.

"Well... We can't drive... Can't walk either. Hey! How 'bout we sneak onto a plane? That's gotta work! Should we do it?"

Bella's face explodes.

I don't answer.

Sneak onto a plane? Well... That could work. Only if we pretend to be different people. Like shorter adults! Yeah, this could work!

I still have a 'maybe face' on. "I'm definitely thinking about it," I explain. "But that sounds like an awesome plan!" I jump up and down and squeal like a typical little girl.

"Ugh. Riley! Why can't you be less grownup-y? Any normal person our age would give me a hard 'no!' Just say it! You probably want to," Bella complains, her sweaty hands on her hips.

I roll my eyes. "Fine."

Chapter Thirteen

The Shortest chapter on the Planet

Dracula was ready to burn Anna. "You muzt vee avle doo burn, now!" *Dracula cackled.*

The piercing sun was scorching on my skin. It was so hot, it could turn someone on fire, literally! (I'm talking about Anna, if you don't know.)

Anna crumbled with fire so much, it looked like she was made of embers and ashes. I wanted to scream, "NOOO!", but she always hated me. This was a harsh decision, but, for Pegsy, I'd do anything. I slowly closed my eyes into Pegasus's pearly coat, but he watched it like it was a horror movie, and he'd just lapped up seven cups of strong coffee. "Anna... was, well, I think pretty scared to burn...but I guess seeing her like this is worse than what we actually maybe could forgive her," Pegasus said. "I actually agree," I said, surprised. "I wouldn't want to be burned to a crisp." Anna is extremely unlucky, and unfortunately, I am too. I guess she did get an unpleasant death.

I sighed. "Oh, Pegsy, sometimes I... kinda wish you were my sibling," I told him.

"I could be your brother... or guardian."

I stared at him. I hugged him so tightly, if he was a water balloon, he would totally burst. "Thank you," I whispered.

Then, Dracula flew toward me! He seized my neck and....

Chapter Fourteen

No More Tomato Faces!

I scream and wake up!

"It <pant> was <pant>..... a <pant> nightmare<pant> the vampires sent." The sheets are all crazily tangled in my two legs. My neck and face are sweaty and I wet the bed!! No high schooler would wet the bed! I change into another pajama bottom and go back to sleep. The nightmare plays again in my head. I say the same words. Pegasus still looks at Anna's burning.

I wake up and take a midnight snack. Cold milk and chocolate chip cookies. It is 3:30 AM and I am still awake! I go back to sleep. I still have the nightmare. The curse is not the best thing ever.... but, a curse is a curse, as Pegsy says. Just a little, I wish that some of that was real. The part where Pegasus says that we can be brother and sister. I sigh. "Could we be siblings?" Nah. Anyway, Pegsy probably wouldn't want to. ...Or would he? Eh, either way, he's already a happy horse -I mean Pegasus. What if I ruin our friendship and turn it into a brother-sister feud? I sigh and play with General Puppy until dawn. I can't handle this nightmare business.

It's now 9:30 AM and I'm looking for the mail. I yawn a long, sound blocking yawn. When I yawn and I'm looking in a mirror, I can see the bottom of my esophagus. I haven't slept since 3:30 AM!!!! I open the mail, drowsily. Anna is still asleep since it's Saturday and she sleeps until 10:00. Wait....she's at Dracula's prison. Maye he decided to let her live, because I can feel it.

I can feel that Anna is *alive.*

I have this strange feeling that she is alive.

I shuffle through the letters. Taxes for Dad, bank stuff for Mom, and car insurance for both of them. They still don't know they're dead?! Oh, never mind. They'll learn soon.

Then... Another letter from Drake Banis. These letters are quagmires! It reads:

I know that you have altered the curse by using Pegasus's Magic. You have not fooled us.

You are a rat, Riley, a rat.

You are powerless as I am powerful.

We will kill Pegasus.

Just you wait, you rotten fleabag.

Just you wait and see with your eyes.

That is horrible! They are gonna kill Pegasus!!! I cannot allow this thing to happen. I cannot allow this thing to happen. I cannot allow this thing to happen.

"I CANNOT ALLOW THIS TO HAPPEN!!!!!!" I howl, tears blurring my vision.

I speed toward Buddy. He whinnies in alarm. I say the turning words. Pegasus appears. "Look! Look! Dracula!" I say frantically. All the drowsiness drains out of my body. Pegasus reads the note and his eyes widen. "Is this—" he starts to say, but I interrupt him by saying,"Pegsy, we have to turn you into Buddy at all times. We can't risk being seen by Dracula. And I have to call you... um, Randy instead of Buddy! And we have to dye you another color! How about....brown? With a blaze marking! So that the vampires can't see you! Oh, Pegasus, please! Don't die! Please!" I say, still crying. Pegasus is speechless. "Ok....." he says, finally. And with a flash, he's Buddy. I hug him, weeping.

After a while, the tears dry out in the July heat. I go to my mom's room. I take the dye that kept her hair brown. I take it all and get to work. I spray, I paint, I put the paste on and hose him down. I even shave some of his hair off to make him look like Bailey, or the talking horse!

I step back, studying my work. Buddy looks completely like Bailey, his friend. I leave a bit of white on his hock. I then wash him with the hose thirty-eight minutes later. Then, I call Bella over and we ride horses. Bella's horse, Sergeant, is kinda.....like Buddy, in his new disguise. Our horses trot in rhythm. "Riley, wasn't Buddy...white? This horse is chestnut," she says, quizzically.

"Oh! Buddy was horrible, so we got another horse. This is Randy," I say, trying not to let the absolute lie show. <Nicker!> Buddy nickers. I think that meant *"Please, Riley! No, I'm perfect! Don't even lie about that!"* I pat Buddy's wide, mane covered neck.

Bella frowns. "Oh." Her hair swings up as Sergeant trots like a red fox. Buddy whinnies. Sergeant nickers back. They trot and move into a smooth canter. Bella and I whoop! This is fun!!!

"Why was Buddy bad?" Asks Bella.

"Oh, you know, killed a maid or two," I say, casually. Bella raises an eyebrow.

"Oh, really? How?"

I hesitate and then say, "Got mad, kicked them straight in the back of their brain. Didn't like people who he didn't know. He even tried doing that to my dad!"

Bella gasps. "That is a terrible horse! I thought Buddy was so sweet!" I try to smile a bit, but it's hard to lie.

Then I whisper, "This *is* Buddy! He *doesn't* kill anyone! There are vampires trying to kill *only him*! You see, when I say, I wish I could see Pegasus, Pegasus appears! But you *cannot* tell anyone. If you do, Pegsy and I are in *huge* trouble!"

I am horrible at keeping secrets.

Just horrible. Don't ask.

Bella's eyes widen. "He is? Then why is he *brown*?"

Is Bella on a quiz show?

"Oh, I have to keep him brown so that Dracula doesn't see him. They want to kill Pegsy." She gasps a breathy gasp. She is about to hyperventilate.

"Calm down," I tell her.

"You *aren't* telling the truth, Ri." Bella convinced herself that I am a liar. I look at her, annoyed.

I sigh. "Come with me," I say, and pull Randy's—Buddy's—reins. "Okay." We turn our brown horses around and we go inside my large mansion. Buddy and Sergeant come in, too. "Are...you, um sure they should....come in? They're ruining the carpet." The truth is...Bel is right. They are ruining the luxurious carpet. The red and white satin carpet that came from the British monarch is covered in muddy horse hooves. "Okay, work your magic, Riley," Bella says.

"Okay. Buddy, I wish I could see Pegasus," I say. A bright light is glimmering Bella's honey brown eyes. Our hair is blowing away. Bella covers her eyes.

"Wow!" she says, loudly and mesmerized. "How can this be *happening?!*"

"Magic," I say, smiling. Bella's long, ginger hair looks like it can tangle in a tree! Then, abruptly, we both crash on the ground. Dizzy, we both get up.

"OMG," Bella says. There is Pegasus, glamorous as ever, still surrounded by the ever so slight bit of a yellow glow.

"Riley, didn't ya say you weren't going to turn me into Pegasus?" he says, raising an eyebrow, if horses have any. Pegasus does a good job of that if horses—magical ones—can.

Bel's red blonde hair curls up and down like slinkies.

"What the......." She groans.

"Is it just my crazy head or is Buddy growing wings and is talking?" she says, stuttering.

"No. No one has crazy heads!" I say, giggling. "Hey, I wish I could see a unicorn!" Bella exclaims, hoping for Sergeant, her horse, to turn into a unicorn.

Well, guess what!

Suddenly, there is a flash of blue light! We slide down the path as it slants like an earthquake! We scream in hope and delight of the thought of Sergeant being a mythical creature. And there is a unicorn! Standing where Sergeant is. I scream again! Sergeant is a unicorn!

"Hey y'all! I'm a unicorn, The name's Amber, I'm a girl, No surprise, since the name's Amber."

Amber is a funny name for a snow white unicorn with a golden horn and a twangy accent similar to Karen's. And she has a set of *wings??* I guess so. Bella runs and hugs Amber. Pegasus... well, he is blushing and flirting??? Oooohhhh........Pegasus and Amber, sitting in a tree, K-I-S-S-I-N-G!

"Pegasus and Amber, sitting in a tree, K-I-S-S-I-N-G! First comes love, then comes marriage and then comes Amber with a horsie carriage!" I giggle into Pegsy's ear.

Pegasus blushes furiously! His entire face is practically pink! He hides his face in his wings.

"Pegsy is smitten," I say the same thing in Bella's ears. She giggles. Bel and I tease them. Then they disappear in a flash! Bella and I beam. We both have an awesome secret! But, we both share the same threat. Dracula. She doesn't know that Dracula's coming after her, so I tell her.

"What???!!!!!!!!" she screams.

"And, also, my parents......died," I tell her.

"From Dracula?" she asks.

I nod.

"I will *kill* that guy!" she vows.

"Yeah, but I need to show you something," I tell her.

Pegasus, Amber, Bella, and I circle around the pile of Drake Banis letters I gathered up. There are more.

"Wow," Amber says.

"This isn't wow. Dracula wants to kill us! Look!" I pick one up.

We will kill you

And we will succeed.

Once we will,

Olympus will be ours.

Jupiter will be powerless

Against us.

So there.

"Blegh! I totally hate him!" Bella comments, shaking her head.

Disgusted, we start a meeting.

"This is terrible, Ri! Why didn't you tell me about it?" Bella asks, kind of disappointed in me.

I sigh. "I don't think anyone's supposed to know."

"I know about this!" Amber scowls. "I heard thousands of people tried to kill him, never succeeded. Instead, *he* killed *them*," she says, in a spooky voice.

Pegsy laughs nonstop. Loud. I mean, like suuuuper *SUPER* loud.

"I like you Amber. You're kinda funny," I say. She smiles, Pegasus still guffawing.

165

"Guys! Focus!" Bella scolds, as almost all of us snapped our attention back. Pegasus is still laughing as hard as possible.

"PEGSY!"

This is nuts.

"And you remember Anna, the maid?" I ask Bella.

"Well duh!" Bella cries.

"Well, Anna is a *traitor. She* is helping Drac. *She* is a vampire. *She* wants to kill us. *She* is going to die. Drac decided to burn her. And it happened. I saw it in my nightmare. My curse *works*. Anna is dead. Dead a vampire. At least that's what I think." I say darkly.

"You have a CURSE!?" Bella gasps. I nod.

I pull down the blinds. The room gets darker.

I gesture to a string, and I tug the slightly damp string.

I put a finger to my lips. "SHHH!"

"WHY?" Bel mouths.

I give her a troll eye glare. "BECAUSE," I mouth.

The string gives way and a ladder unfolds.

"Do not make a sound! The wild creature will attack you!" I whisper.

We climb up the creaky steps.

166

Pegsy has a little trouble but he shrinks! And he buzzes up and into the room, or cramped attic that is very ancient. Oh man! Did my parents just blow their money getting the mansion?! I hear growling.

'Pegsy! Psst! Make a shield that won't let any sound escape?' I hiss. Pegsy nods, and a big bubble erupts out of the ground, soundlessly. It closes around us with a *WHOOSH*, and all is silent. I gesture toward a podium speech thingy. It has lots of Drake Banis letters.

"Look at this letter," I say, holding up a letter:

We hate you.

You will not ever hesitate

To the question of vampires ever again.

The answer should be yes. Yes. Yes. Yes.

"What the—"

"This is, by far, the strangest letter we've received yet!" Pegasus exclaims.

"This is horrible!" Bella shrieks.

"I've seen worse," I say.

"But what does he mean 'The question of the vampires'? What even *is* that?"

167

"All I know is that this is dangerous, and that you need to be protected," Bella says.

"Uh-huh... Do you think the question of the vampires is 'Who are they?'" I ask, totally ignoring Bella.

"Nah, why would the answer be 'Yes'? That doesn't make sense," Amber explains.

"True..." I agree.

"Everything you say is true, Amber!!" Pegasus blurts. We all look at him.

"Awk-ward!" I whisper to Bella.

"Boy, you are so right!" Bella says, shaking her head.

"Get a room, lovebirds!" Bella cries.

"Love *horses,*" I correct her.

Pegsy and Amber get their attention span back in a few minutes, and I keep reading the mysterious letters.

After a while, Bella begins to understand that her mom was killed by vampires.

"...And not only do I need to be protected, but *you* do, too! Maybe even more than me!" I advise her.

"I'm pretty independent," Bella says, stubborn as a goat.

"Listen, Bella, I know you're upset this might happen, but you *have to listen to me!* You aren't safe. I can go to Olympus. You can, too," I explain.

"But my dad is still alive. He's not supposed to know, I thought," she says, still a little annoyed and stubborn.

"Smart thinking. If they are still alive, you may tell them."

"Bella," I begin, "I have bad news. We can't be together anymore after this vampire stuff. You see, Amber has to go back to the Unicorn World, you too. Pegsy and I have to go to Olympus. We cannot be together," I say, sadly. Pegsy still perks up.

"Wait! The portal, called The Portal, ha ha, can bring us to the Unicorn world. I have been there before and—"

"Then Pegasus and I can stay together!" cheers Amber, interrupting Pegsy.

Pegsy turns the color of a tomato.

"I guess... If you really *want* to..." he says, blushing, and turning a shade of red.

Bella and I exchange a grossed-out look. "Look who's in lo-ove!" I say, laughing my head off.

"Pegsy is smitten!"

"Ewww!" Bella nods, but giggles. I just shake my head.

"Wait, can we call our crazy lovestruck horses back to normal? You know, Sergeant and Buddy?"

"I know! You just say, 'Can Buddy or Sergeant come back.' And then we become horses," says Amber.

We do.

There are our horses. Buddy and Sergeant. *Phew!*

Chapter Fifteen

Work

Bella rides home to her farmland house and I am flopping on my bed. My head is hurting. What if Bella tells the truth? She wouldn't do that. Plus, her mom is dead. Poor Bel.

Never mind. Let me check the mail.

Taxes, taxes, more taxes and car insurance. Why don't they know? The mail is clogged with taxes and angry letters. I step back, to see the marble mailbox starting to lean over. Woah!

I fish out a letter marked : IMPORTANT, OPEN RIGHT NOW!! To Riley E. Peterson. From *Drake Banis*. Now, *that's* a letter. I hope bats don't suddenly fly out of the envelope! Or someone saying, "Mwa ha ha! Greetings, Riley Foolishness, you are about to die, you dummy! Ha! In your face! So there!" Ewww! I hate even Imaginary Dracula!

With trembling hands, I carefully open the letter.

We dislike your plans more than we would like

Bathing in a pool of garlic on a sunny day with

Wooden stakes surrounding us. Believe me, that,

Some day your heart will be

Pricked by a thorn on a rosebush. You will scream in agony. You will sleep

for 100 years.

You will be the most hated human beings on Earth.

You'll see.

That is horrible! Though the Sleeping Beauty part was a little funny. I must warn Bella and Amber and Pegsy! Wait, better to keep Amber and Pegsy...apart. Don't wanna know how much trouble, or awkwardness, they could cause.

They'd blush and stammer and other stuff.........

I rush inside the house and call Bella on my pink cell phone on the table. I dial the number, and then

"Bel,....yeah....hi....this is important.....Drake Banis....a letter......do not turn Sergeant into Amber....yes....ha ha......ok....bye."

172

I try to hold the letter in my shaking hands and try to read. It's hard with such shaky hands. Bella is there in five seconds flat. She is very punctual. She reads the creepy letter.

"This is horrible! I truly hate Dracula! Should I bring Amber and you call Pegsy? I'm sure they could help."

"Help make an awkward moment, ahem," I say, rolling my eyes.

"They might not, you never know," she protests in a soft, melodic voice. Her curls bounce up and down. And in two flashes, Pegsy and Amber emerge. They turn the color of tomatoes when they look at each other. Okay....
Off to a bumpy start...

"Ahem," I clear my throat and walk over to the mythical creatures.

"There will be no turning into tomatoes, blushing, flirting, or any awkward business. 'Kay?" I ordered, pulling the bottom of my tee shirt.

"I can't promise that," sighs Pegsy, deeply and madly in love.

Amber just stares at him, lost in thought.

"Hey! Ambie! I know that you're focusing on your crush, and that is important, but we gotta focus! Amber!

173

Amber?" Bella tells her, really irritated. She takes a step back. "Hm..?---WHA?!" Amber asks, finally jolting awake from her trance.

"You were right. I really shouldn't have let these guys come along," Bella admits.

I nod my head proudly. "Mmm-hmm"

"Hi... I ... like-your-wings," Amber compliments Pegasus, shyly.

"*Thank* you!! Thank you, thank you, so, so much!" Pegasus hollers. "I-I mean, thanks." He calms down. I roll my eyes.

"Oh, boy."

Twenty minutes, and we're *finally* getting to the point.

"If Anna is a vampire, and she lives with you, she may know that Buddy is Pegasus. If she has told Dracula, then the vampires may already know. I think that the vampires are doing something big," Bella hypothesizes.

Her hands are laced in one another.

We kept the horses as our beloved pets, Buddy and Sergeant.

"I already know their plan. They want to attack this very beautiful mansion. They are going to kill Pegsy. Probably tomorrow or *today*. We have to be prepared for this attack. Set up sneaky booby traps. *This is life or death,*" I state.

"Yes. This is so bad, I think Amber and Pegsy... *may not survive* if we do not be prepared. Let's get to work. Now." She rises and snaps her fingers, giving orders. "Amber! Quit flirting with Pegsy! You and I will build traps! And Ri! Keep Pegsy away from Amber! You two make garlic traps, so the vampires fall into the garlic and die--well evaporate, 'kay?" She barks.

Bel has really changed.

We saw, we hammer, we dig.

This was the most lugubrious work ever!

Amber and Pegsy are helping, but are kept apart.

Pegsy helps me with the ginger traps. Amber and Bel make the wooden stake traps. Pegsy and I dig like crazy.

Pegsy with his beautiful golden hooves and me with my mom's tough gardening shovel. I am sweating like crazy. If you collected all my sweat, mine would be bigger than the salty Pacific Ocean.

Finally after a billion minutes I pant to Pegsy,

"Pe<pant>gs<pant>y<pant>, let's<pant> take a<pant>break."

175

I pat the cool ground, motioning Pegasus to sit down.

He does. He looks like a big dog when he's sitting down on his haunches.

"I really think that this is unnecessary, Riley. I am immortal! Wait, is Amber immortal? If not, then this is completely necessary, Riley! *Completely.*"

Pegasus looks worried.

I laugh.

"Come on, tomato. Sit down and quit talking about Amb. Don't worry about it, we're nice and safe. Anyway, she and Bella are working hard on it," I insist to him, comfortingly.

"I think I should help them..." he starts.

"Nope!" I add, yanking on his long tail.

"Hey!" he whinnys.

"Get your big butt down here. NOW!" I scold him.

He strains to get a glimpse of Amber's pointy golden horn from afar, before flopping down with a *thud*! I cough, as stinky dust storms come up from his butt and into my nose.

He farted.

"Well, ok. But Riley, please! I don't see what's wrong with talking to Amber. That beautiful, fun... lovable..." he starts.

"I'll tell ya what's wrong! What's *wrong* is that you two will start blushing and rambling on and on and on about your stupid comments and you never say a single 'I love you'!" I explain.

"B-because I can't! I can't tell her my feelings for her! I'm too embarrassed!" he admits, sobbing his heart out.

"Don't look at me!"

I pat his back.

"Dude. She already knows," I tell him, insensitively.

"And she knows, she loves you, too. We're teasing her about it. Same as you."

"You sure?" he asks, praying for me to be right. I nod my head, reassuringly.

"Oh, joy! Oh, happy day!!! Oh, wonderful life!" He happily sings and prances around mom's red rose garden. He accidentally tramples on a flower. I pluck one beautiful bloomed red rose and hand it to him.

"Here, give this to Am. Go!" I pat his rump. He hesitates and then prances to Amber.

...

Bel and Amber were sweating like it was a million degrees out. But they kept on sawing and sawing. Amber used her own horn! What if it fell off?! Bella had insisted that she use her magic powers, but Amber, stubborn as a goat, demanded using her horn. Bella used a saw from her father's tool kit.

Her father had left this behind before moving to the northern part of Nova Scotia, Canada. He left the handy dandy tool kit behind since thirteen year old Bella loved to build and experiment things. Ever since she was five. She and her dad used to build a building with blocks for hours. Bella wanted to be an architect. Dad was in Canada, being an engineer.

Bella tried to show her mom she was recovering from the divorce. Her parents fought for hours. Ms Hamilton broke her ankle in one of the fights. He'd twisted it and.....

Bella actually, was full of despair and wasn't keeping up with her studies. Her grades were low. Around minus B or a C in every subject, well besides art. It kept all her worries washed out of her mind and into the sea of worries, far away into the edges of the colossal, dark universe.

Vampires.

What were they doing now?

What were the obnoxious, single minded, foul vampires doing?

Were they poking and prodding her mother's body, trying to find the very life giving place in her? Her heart? Or were they burning her? There was one word for vampires.

Cruel.

Her mind was screaming in agony every time something reminded of her dad or mom.

And now, after the nasty vampires had killed her, Bella was as lonely as ever. Like a forgotten thing, at the very bottom of the deep blue sea.

This was a very rotten month. Well besides knowing that Sergeant was a unicorn, Amber.

Sensing her thoughts, Amber paused from gluing a plank of timber with her pure unicorn magic and tapped her long, golden horn on Bella's shoulder. All the sadness drained from Bella!

"I know this is hard for you right now. You'll be okay with a unicorn by your side, though. You are *okay*," Amber said, and set her head down on Bella's sweaty lap.

"Thank you." Bella smiled, tears disappearing from her eyes forever.

"Maybe I'll take a little break. You should, too, Amber."

Amber grinned, extremely relieved that Bella needed a rest.

"This was fun, darling," she said, sweating in the burning Texas heat.

Even though unicorns don't have sweat glands. That's just how hot it was!

"And, I used my unicorn magic to make your divorce problems disappear in a puff. I wonder what sweet Pegsy is doing. I wish he was here." She blushed once.

Clomp, clomp. Pegsy emerged from a clump of wet, dewed bushes.

"Your wish is my command, my Princess Amber!" He was clutching a beautiful *rose* in his teeth.

"My wonderful prince charming Pegsy! What a wonderful and pleasant surprise! Wow!!!! Roses! My favorite!"

"Ooohhh. Pegsy and Amber, sitting in a tree, K-I-S-S-I-N-G!" Bella sang, laughing her head off.

Then, Pegsy said it. "I L-O-V-E *love* you!"

"Blegh!!!" Bella choked out.

"Gross!!"

Amber's face lit up and she nearly fainted!

"Oh, dearest Pegsy! I love you, too!" she admitted, her voice breaking.

"Okay, Romeo and Juliet. Break it up, and get back to work!" Bella ordered, with great irritation.

Pegsy trotted back, looking over his withers, grinning.

I sigh, watching the moment. Gross.

Weird.

I get back to work. Ten minutes later, it's one foot deep. I dash into the kitchen and gather all the garlic in the pantry. I also take a long, long, super long drink of cooling water. Ahhh...so refreshing! I dash back and dump the pile of essential vampire slaying machines. I need this. Duh! Pegsy finally comes back and with a flash, is Buddy. He whinnies and starts making a pile of leaves by plucking one from a tree next to us. I sigh and walk over into the cool shade as my hair billows in the July wind. Buddy turns into Pegasus when I say the magic words.

"Wow, Riley. Ready for a nap *already*?" Bel teases.

"What can I say? I'm a tired person!" I announce and pretend to snore.

"Finally!" Pegasus yells, smashing his face straight into the fence. He lifts his head, which is full of splinters

181

(YEESH) and stampedes to the 'Glorious Amber'. I slap my hand on my head. This IS gonna be one looooong day.

Chapter Sixteen

Anna the Traitor, was very rude and rotten! She

died a death of fi-i-re and was forgo-o-tten!

(Frosty the Snowman remix)

Beads of sweat trickle down my face. I take a sip of water. \<sigh\> I hang the crosses all over the house. The house seems unusually warm. No. *Hot* is more like it. I am as scorching as all the stars in the Milky Way and more universes. I wonder why. Is something happening to our house? Global warming? I refill my empty water bottle. There isn't a single drop of water in the water bottle.

I drink it all clean in just a microsecond. I hope the water supply isn't going away. I climb up the staircase.

 I then go to the secret door to the roof. No one knows this door. Not even Bella or Pegsy. You go to my room, open the closet, go behind the Trunk of Memories to find the door.

Open it, and climb up the neatly polished, never used stairs, to the roof. I then remove one tile each on the roof. One tile by another, I come to the planks of wood. I get a few splinters, but I ignore the pain and start to saw the planks away with an electric saw.

Ten centuries later, I stop. I then carefully, with a chisel, pick away at the nails. I come down the secret door to find a picture of my mom and dad that got slipped out of the Trunk Of Memories. I snatch the photograph from the wooden floor. It was when they were on their honeymoon. My mom had long, curly reddish brown hair with a hint of blonde and almond-shaped eyes the color of caramel. She looked kind of like how I would imagine Bella as a grown-up. My dad had jet black hair that kinda started to gray. His green eyes are glowing with happiness. I miss him so much. He was so funny. And my mom was so smart. I hold this photo to my chest like when I hold General Puppy sometimes. I then race into my room and pin it on my corkboard with photographs and sketches. Then, I go upstairs to the wrecked roof and get back to work.

Meanwhile, Bella and Amber started digging more holes that day. "Maybe it's time we add the garlic, Bella," Amber said, finally.

"I've been waiting for you to say that! Amber, I was waiting for eternity!!" Bella gushed, her clear Boston accent more tired than ever.

She ran to Amber. Amber assured that Bella's gone crazy.

"I've been digging holes for ages!! Ages!!! AGES!!!!!" Bella was acting very weird at the time, so Amber insisted she go inside for a water break.

She took a little tiny sip of it.

"Ahhhh.... Waaaaater....." she sighed. "Sweet, wonderful *WATER!!*"

She went into the refrigerator and took a piece of garlic and bit right into it!

"Mmm--" she moaned. But then, a sour look began spreading across her face.

"AAAAAHHHH!" she screamed. Amber sighed and rolled her eyes, refusing to watch Bella make a fool of herself and running around the room.

"I wonder if she needs to go to a hospital," she exaggerated. They came outside.

"Is it just me, or do I see a penguin?" Bella asked.

"The sun is playing tricks on you. 'Kay? Sit under the shade. I'll work," Amber said, with her soft, angelic voice. She still sounded kind of annoyed, though.

I hear my ringtone going off. It's a call from... Unknown? Ignore. I have better things to do than to answer a prank call. I go back to my work. I keep on sliding out planks of timber wood. The nails are gone from where I chipped them off. Then I undo the wires. I use electricity proof gloves and pick away at the electric, dangerous wires.

Ding! Ding! A voice message from Mr. Banis. Mr. Banis!? I listen to it.

"This is Drake Banis. We dislike you. We know your plan, and we will ruin it. We will destroy you and your winged friends. We shall end them and your lives! Mwa ha ha!!" He says, evilly.

"This is serious. This is no joke. I have to tell Bella. Now," I mutter. I dash over to where Bella's dozing in the cooling shade.

"Bella! Bella! Wake up!" I jolt her awake.

"Yeah?? -What's goin' on?" she groans. "I was sleeping."

"This! Look!" I cry frantically. I replay the message. The 'Mwa ha ha' burns like acid, ruining my brain as it echoes in my mind. I shudder.

"Bella, check your mail. Now. He knows Amber exists. Let's see if you get any Drake Banis letters. Let's go. You go, but make sure Ambie is Sergeant. We can't risk these dudes getting lost. The fate of them will make us responsible if we leave them alone."

"Yeah! These guys are wicked awesome!"

I pat her on the back. She walks away, forgetting the undoing words. I say for both of them and with a flash, they are horses again. I sigh in fright of losing the two poor horses. I could see it already: getting chased by the victorious vampires... Pegasus grunting in pain... Amber shrieking in absolute agony as she tries to slash the vampires with her pointy horn but fails, swarmed by the bloody monsters. Anxiety crawls through my delicate soul. My nerves are shaking up my tense body. I mustn't let this happen!

We spend the next few hours working on defensive stuff. A pot or a shiny, hard pan bang on a head would daze a wicked vampire. We arm ourselves with homemade DIYs. Then we make giant catapults. We load them with blinding shiny gold crosses, and giant spikes so that their cloaks would come down and the vampires would fall. Then their 'things' that kept the sun from burning them wouldn't work.

We cut, we hammer, we glue, and we sweat! We all take drinks of water until the water bottle is dry to the bone. Buddy is nearly fainting from the heat! We have to leave them in the cooling shade.

The soft breeze tickles his short coat. His long, fake chestnut mane is flying all over the place as the windy air hits his fake brown hair.

We haul the two catapults onto the roof. We really are damaging this beautiful house. Oh well. It is for the sake of Pegsy. And Amber.

Buddy whinnies. His brown coat is a bit matted since I didn't brush him in a while. Heh heh. I smile, and jump down the high roof. "RILEY!" Bel screams.

I land flat on my bottom. "I'm OKAY!" I say.

What am I thinking?!

I see Buddy's eyelids droop down, down, down until they are closed and he is fast asleep. He dozes onto the soft, long grass.

"Awww..." I coo, quietly. I kiss him on the top of his head.

"Hi!" Bella greets me. Surprised, I jump up and hold my right fist out to her like I am about to punch her. She successfully dodges my attempt. My eyes twitch. I thought she was Dracula! I hold my hand tightly.

I chuckle nervously. This is *so* embarrassing!

"I'm so *so* sorry, Bella! I actually thought you were a vampire!" I apologize.

"Nervous energy, eh? It's cool. I'm having *fun* building these traps! I'm like a mini builder! That's what my old man calls me," she says, proud of herself.

"Yeah," I agree, still a bit of guilt in my voice about what I'd just almost done to her.

"'Kay. I gotta tell you a thing. This is... A private girl conversation." Bella is already giggling before she even ends her sentence!

"As I was saying," Bella still has her giggling fits, "this is a private girl conversation. So, did you know that Pegasus said he wants a date with Amber?"

Olympians don't go on dates. I glance over at Buddy and Sergeant. They are *nuzzling* muzzles! Ewwwww!!!

"Aw, that's actually kinda cute!" Bella sings songs, in a sort of high-pitched voice.

"I mean, you gotta admit. They *are* pretty adorable when they're horses."

I nod my head.

"Weird, huh? Olympians rarely even fall in love, except Cupid, and Apollo. And Aphrodite. They don't even know dates or stuff. We should teach them that. We have to stop this awkwardness. We can't do this when the vamps come. What if they keep on doing this stuff and the vampires attack and they die? And when we have to leave Earth and go to their worlds, these guys will be horribly inseparable! We won't be able to leave Earth!" I cry.

I storm off to Buddy. I turn him into Pegsy.

"Pegsy, I have to tell you something." I lecture to him that this is just a silly crush. There will be consequences if he doesn't stop. With a flash, Amber appears. I tell her the same thing.

"Here, on Earth, Olympus, the unicorn world, and anywhere else, there is no blushing, or anything lovely dovely. Okay? No more anything like that. There will be no way you can do things like this. Per-i-od," I lecture them, in a really serious voice.

"Okay, okay. Fine, I won't do this 'Stupid weird stuff' anymore." Pegsy says.

"Ms. Bossy," he mumbles, softly, under his breath. I just ignore him and thunder over to Amber.

"Amber. No more like this. Do you hear me!? Do you hear?!" I am officially an army general. Like General Puppy but not a dog.

"Bella and I are the official generals and chiefs here. Everyone is going to listen to us." The two majestic animals nod solemnly.

"Repeat after me and raise your right wing. I Pegasus or Amber, do solemnly swear,"

"I, Pegasus and Amber do solemnly swear," They buzz in unison.

"We will never ever blush, or do any lovey dovey stuff,"

"We will never ever blush or do any lovey dovey stuff,"

"Ever again in my life or there will be consequences,"

"Ever again in my life or there will be consequences,"

"Enforced by Bella Hamilton and Riley Peterson."

"Enforced by Bella Hamilton and Riley Peterson. " They finish. They lower their wings.

I look more closely at Amber's wings. They are cartoonish and small. They don't have a giant wingspan like how Pegsy's majestic huge wings with a wide wingspan as

191

large as a California Condor's is. Wait...bigger than a California Condor. Wow. They almost, almost, *drag* on the floor.

They do not blush when they look at each other. I pull Pegsy away and whispcr to him. "Pegsy! How in the world did you know about dates?"

"Oomph"

I clamp my palm around his drooling mouth, yuck, and hush, "Do you hear that?" Everyone stills. *Tap, tap, tap. Tap!*

Many, many footsteps!

"Dracula's army," I whisper.

We dash into the spacious house and arm ourselves with the homemade defenses. Then, we silently tiptoe to the roof. I slide the chest behind the secret door against it so that they can't find the entrance. The door is wide enough for the horses to pass. The chest is huge!

I then throw my best and longest dresses to hide it even more. We slowly and carefully climb the winding stairs to the plank covered roof. From the gaps in the roof, I hear groans of agony. Yes! The trap worked! The main thing was, the vampires would think it was safe to take off their cloaks or 'stuff' that kept the sunlight off of them, and the 'deadly' sunlight streaming in would burn them.

I peer down the roof very carefully. The leaf piles Pegsy made are perfect! Vampires are dropping into the booby traps and black steam is wafting up.

I carefully rise and load up two of the four catapults with garlic and the one with crosses, and other with spikes. Perfect! I also load my shirt and jean pockets with garlic and ready my slingshot. Aahha. I see a vampire flying in the air. Dracula! I flash a grin to Bella, gesturing.

"Dracula," I mouth.

She grins and she fires at other vampires with her slingshot. I fire at Dracula. I hit my bitter enemy target! He disappears in a smokey flash.

I sigh. Finally! He is dead!

A vampire looks up to not see their leader. A flash of recognition appears in my mind as I see her. Anna. HOW IN THE WORLD DID ANNA LIVE!?!?!?!? I grit my teeth. I grind my molars against each other, as I clench my fists into balls. My knuckles turn white. ANNA IS A TRAITOR AND IS ALIVE!!!! I remember her voice like syrup on pancakes.

"Riley. Petersssson...." Anna hisses, in her harshest version of her voice as she glances up to the roof. "Vhy must you be here, Misssss Terrible?! Vhy are you *here*??" She hisses like a king cobra.

"Sssssssssssssssssssssssss......" She looks at Bella, grinning, her fangs gleaming and dripping with green, gooey venom. Is she part snake, bat, *and* vampire!?

"Bella Hamilton... vell vell vell."

I jump in front of Bella.

"Leave her alone!" I cry. " AND YOU ARE A *TRAITOR*." I roar like a lion.

Anna's drool spills out, but then, she notices Pegasus. Her eyes pop out of her head!

"Pigasseessss! Vhat a tasssty treat!!" She smiles, evilly. I run to Pegsy. I hug his neck tightly, tighter than ever!!

"No! Don't hurt him!" I yell, all my rage coming out.

"Vhat are you doing? No!" Anna shouts. I can't say anything. I am very, very angry. Then, Pegsy touches his feathered wing on my forehead. I raise one hand. A beam of fire shoots out! I pull it in and focus. I have to destroy Anna. But I can't! **'You got this, Riley. You are strong.'** Pegsy reassures me in my mind. I roar. I sound like a real lion. All the fighting pauses.

Bella roars with confidence.

She sounds like a polar bear.

Anna hisses. "Sssssssssssss........."

I roar again.

I rage. Then, I take a deep breath, and fire. Straight at Anna.

Chapter Seventeen

The End Of The Anna Era

Fire shoots out of my steady hands. It hits a panicked Anna in her malevolent beating heart. She disappears in a smokey flash.

I contract my hand to my chest. How in the world did I get these powers? I guess it was Pegsy. Seeing my astonished face, Pegsy says, "This is nothing of my powers. This comes from *you*."

Bella tries doing the same and ice shoots out!

"As Pegsy said, the powers come from us, and I really do like ice." Bella stands defiant.

"And I like the fire and the heat. Since I sounded like a lion, and you sound like a polar bear, we got our powers!" I grin.

I then snap back to attention. I keep on firing and launch the catapults.

An absolutely good thing we made catapults since it is working! But Bella's purple ice is not working against the vampires. The freezing ice bolts just bounce off the vampires and shatter as if vampires are made of marble. The frost and snow doesn't work!

I fire at every single vampire. One vampire, two vampires...................................
three......7..................17...........27...........57.....................77...
.........107....117.......127.......... 177....All of them! Bella and I look at each other just like when we first saw Cutie. I wonder where she is. We all cheer happily at our victory.

"OH. MY. GOSH. Guys! Do you realize what this even *MEANS*?! WE KILLED THE VAMPIRES THAT KILLED MY MOM!!!!!! AND RILEY'S PARENTS!!!!! This HAS to be the BEST DAY EVER!!!" Bella shouts.

"Woo-hoo! I think I know what the question of the vampires was. *Will we get defeated by your cleverness?* Of course they will!"

This is even *more* than "Woo-hoo!" This is amazing! It's brilliant! We literally just *killed* the people who killed my parents and Bella's mom! And hurt Pegsy! And sent us all those mean letters! WE MUST CELEBRATE!!!

This is *great! Greater* than great!

Then a boulder rolls in my chest.

We have to go.

Not to the bathroom, knucklehead! (Sorry, I am just… <sniff> going through some things now.)

Why do I always have to be the party pooper?!

We have to be separated now! Bella and Amber will go to the Unicorn world! We, Pegsy, General Puppy and I, will go to Olympus! But we can't be separated! We are BFFS! We were best friends when we were, well, zero. Then Bella moved here, and after a month, fortunately, I moved too.

We're *family*.

But I know we have to go to separate places.

Bella nods unhappily, all the happiness drains out. Except for one little spark, a small firework inside us, telling us that we will *always* be together, never separated, never apart no matter what the case. We will *always* stay strong *together*. We climb on our horses, give a huge, strong, suffocating bear hug, and say, "We will always stay strong, be together in our hearts." We take out our friendship necklaces which we always carry with each other, do our special secret oath no one but us is allowed to hear, tear up a little, and fly away. I think Bel screams something, but I can't hear her because we're too far away.

Bella becomes a dot after a while and so does my former mansion.

This is it. Fun times we had in this big ol' house of ours.

I would miss it a bunch, but this is important. I have to do this, and I am happy for Bella and Amber! I'm just glad that we're all safe. Our new life will be fun. A fresh start for all of us.

General Puppy yips on top of a flying Pegsy.

"General Puppy, stop! I cannot fly in this situation. The departure of one of our generals is making me somber and you are making it even harder!" Pegsy complains.

I stifle a giggle. Pegsy glares at General Puppy. General Puppy yips a happy *ARF!* I love these two! I ruffle General Puppy's wrinkly ears. I also touch Pegsy's feathered wings.

I lie down carefully on Pegsy's back.

We get closer and closer to the fluffy clouds. I zoom up to a straight sitting position. A portal opens up! Pegsy zooms in.

"AHHH!!!!" I scream.

"No need to worry," Pegsy smiles. The Portal sucks us in.

"How can you land on Olympus? You might land on another planet!" I scream over the torturing noise of The Portal.

"The Portal brings you to the planet or world you are living on, so it never makes a mistake!" Pegsy yelled back.

"But then my dog and I are from Earth!" I holler back.

"You can tell The Portal where to go, and then that's the world you are going to!!!!" Pegasus yells back.

I hammer him with questions, but he can't hear! This huge portal is waaaay too loud. And dark. Once I get kind of used to it, I grasp on to Pegsy's wings, shut my eyes like a sealed chest, hold on tight, and enjoy the purple darkness of the ride. Stars are everywhere. Like a nightly cave.

Thump! We land in a majestic, beautiful marble palace. It is a lot like a mansion, but much much *much* larger than my puny mansion.

"Who is it?" booms a voice. Then a big man, twenty feet tall, comes into the room, no, a large....area in the palace. The room is at least like Central Park's size but times four. I'd look like a grain of sand compared to this place!

The Olympian wind blows gently on my face. He is wearing a robe and a wreath of olive leaves? Pegsy straightens.

"Jupy! Jupiter! Here is Jupiter, my uncle!" Pegsy beams. The leader of the gods scoops Pegsy into a crushing bear hug. Pegasus shoots up to 18 feet high, and then, POOF! Yellow sparkles swirl around me, as a watch-like thing pops up onto my hand.

"So now you can be our size. Press the purple and white swirly button," Pegasus says.

I carefully press it, and SHWEEP! I'm 13 feet tall.

"Pegasus! My nephew! You are here! And who is this young lady out here?"

He raises an eyebrow.

"Oh, sorry, sorry," I curtsy and straighten. "I am Riley, Riley Peterson. Pegsy is my buddy, and we were fighting Dracula and his vampires." I introduce myself, with a story to go with it...

The whole time, Jupiter seems to *know* me. He surveys me, looks at me strangely, and just...*knows* me.

He's seen me before. I have a feeling of that.

I haven't seen him though.

"Dracula?! The scoundrel? Oh, I see, there was a large battle. There are bloodstains on your clothes. What kind are they, since on Olympus, Olympians prefer to wear tunics, and the very rich, I am one of them but most rich, wear *robes*."

"Oh! I come from Earth and these clothes are called *shirts, pants/jeans*. Earth has changed. Now stuff is more different and so are the clothes." I smile. I feel so wise teaching an Olympian about something!

"But the last time I visited Earth, people wore tunics. They worshiped us. They built temples in honor of us. Now when Hercules visited a few times ago, the temples were gone. And what are shirts, pants, or jeans?" he asks, curiously.

"I'll tell you later, but I really need a tunic. Juno isn't going to be very happy, since I want to meet her," I gush out.

Zero seconds later, I am right in front of her! Wow! Juno is here! She is stunning. Her brown hair is neatly combed. She is also twenty feet tall.

I can hardly breathe.

"I can't breathe."

"That's right, my dear. Breathing is for babies," she says, in a very calm and gentle voice. Her voice is like thick maple syrup, dripping wavily on a stack of pancakes, or waffles or something. How could she keep her tone like that?!

"Huh?" I ask with confusion.

"Here, on Olympus, you don't need to breathe! Nothing will happen. As I speak, I'm not breathing," she explains. She sounds like a motivational speaker or a politician even saying that one sentence.

"Really? Not one breath? *Ever?!*"

"Nope."

I am astonished at this statement, but just go with it. My lungs don't do any work at all at that moment.

I don't breathe.

"Wow! I may never breathe again!"

Juno smiles graciously.

"The wonders of Olympus, right?" she says, pointing to all the beautiful sights in this total palace. She looks like an angel smiling. Seriously, light effects? She's got it all.

She's amazing.

"And The Portal can open up to the Unicorn World!" Jupiter adds.

203

"Unicorn world! I need to go there! My friend, Bella, is there! We need to go there! And have you seen Amber, the unicorn?" The words tumble out of my happy mouth.

"Oh, yes! She is the chief of jokes and is loaded with funny jokes." Jupiter laughs.

I smile. "May we please go to the Unicorn world? *Pleeease*?" I plead.

I do the puppy dog trick. It goes like this. You kinda frown and make your eyes real big and innocent and raise both your eyebrows. Then you make puppy sounds. *<whine!> <whine!>*

"No. This is for the safety of Pegasus and you. You are not going to whine about this. The end," Jupiter scolds firmly.

I tried calling Bella. **'No range'** the phone reads.

"Ugh!" I groan.

"What?" Juno asks.

"Bella. I tried calling her, but it has no range. And what's the time?"

"There is no time on Olympus. We Olympians do not track time, months, or years. We also do not speak English," Juno explains.

"Then how can I understand you and you understand me?" I exclaim.

"When you are on another world, you speak their language and you can understand them," Juno explains.

Oh.

General Puppy yips and Juno and Jupiter jump.

"Aaahhh!! Cruel, cruel world!!!" Jupiter screams his insensitive, offending heart out. "Die! DIE!!!!"

"What *is* this *disgusting* creature?!" They almost gag.

"That is a dog. You know, cute, adorable, they lick you." General Puppy gives a wet lick on my cheek. "They also are very lovable and loyal. Other dogs are not as wrinkled as General Puppy," I explain. "He and Cerberus might be related."

"Oh, I thought that was a demon!" Juno sighs in relief.

A girl, seventeen feet tall, strolls in. She has deep flowing black hair, and a silver tunic. She has a tiara in her hair and a hunting bow is slung over her shoulder. Her deer are tagging along beside her.

"Who is this puny girl?" she asks, in a very disturbed tone.

She looks strong.

"Diana, pay some respect, my daughter. This is Pegasus's companion. She also calls Pegasus—" starts Juno.

Diana interrupts Juno in mid sentence. "I'm not your daughter! I'm your *other non-daughter!* Latona is my mother! Be more aware of my bloodline, right, *Juno?*" she asks sweetly to Juno.

"Oh, yes, yes," Juno says, rolling her eyes. "Sometimes she can be quite nasty," she whispers to Pegsy and I.

"I *heard* that!" Diana scoffs. "You see what I mean?" she says to me.

"Mmm........yeah..." I whisper, shyly. A little confused. I like this lady.

"Only *my* mom is kind to me, as she understands me best and so I like her best," she whispers back. One of her Khrysokeroi deer nods in agreement.

'I agree, child.'

I stumble backwards.

"What's wrong?" Diana asks.

"I-I, I heard your deer talk! She said," I start imitating the deer's voice. " '*I agree, child.*' "

"You. Are. Nuts! Only the gods or demigods can understand *my* deer!" Diana says, but there is a hint of recognition in her voice. She *knows* me!

206

I take a good look at Diana. She looks like she is around twenty-two and has raven black hair. She is super strong. She has muscles.

Cool.

"Have you seen Cerberus?" I ask curiously.

"Oh yes! I have *trained* him. I took the Hellhound cakes that Uncle Pluto—not Mickey Mouse's dog, but the leader of the underworld—gave me to tame that three headed beast." Diana laughs. "That was too easy."

A few "hours" later, we are sitting in Pegsy's private garden.

"Pegsy, I want to see your golden bridle," I say, looking at his pearly white face.

"Why?"

"I want you to try it on," I answer.

"Why?"

"'Cause."

"Why? You aren't going to control me like Bellerophon controlled me, are you?" says Pegsy, raising an eyebrow.

He flies away.

"Pegsyyyyyyyy!" I groan. "Ugh!"

Later that day, Jupiter conjures a room for me, and it is bigger than our grand ballroom back on Earth! He shows me a wardrobe in which seamstresses have stuffed as many clothes as there would take to make another of my friends (She lives in California now) squeal with joy. It has tunics, T-shirts, jeans, and just 5 dresses. I explained the jeans, shirts, and other clothes and that stuff after I dressed for the evening, to Jupiter. A shirt and shorts. The dresses look more like ball gown dresses. Ugh. I swear, I *will not* touch 'em in my life, unless we go for a big giant ball.

I have a canopy bed, tropical blue of course, and a very large comfy luxury dog bed fit for a mastiff puppy (General Puppy, of course) which is filled with chew toys.

I've managed to get my diary along with me, so I keep it on a bookshelf.

The bathroom is the size of a typical living room. There is a marble countertop, with little drawings of dolphins. The mirror is with a gold frame and is massive.

That night, I have the best sleep I've ever had in my life.

Bella was astonished at the Unicorn World! There were white unicorns with colorful manes everywhere! The sky was constantly pink. The clouds were made of cotton candy! The lollipop trees swayed in the sweet popcorn smelling breeze. Delicious mouth watering aromas filled Bella's nostrils with joy. She looked around the breathtaking sights. She was swept away by the artwork and graffiti left on the strong brick walls. "Aaaaahhh....." Bella sighed. "Everything is so quiet.—"

"Yet so many things are happening," Amber finished, looking around in awe.

"Exactamundo." Bella smiled. She lay on a peaceful spot in the swaying grass and shade. *Simply wonderful!* She thought, *I'm so lucky I get to live here!* Bella got to the boardwalk, amazed!

"Yep. This is my home!!!!" she assured herself, as soon as she realized that she could actually eat clouds. "You live here!? It's amazing!" Bella helped herself by gobbling up chunks of clouds that ventured farther than the other clouds. She stuffed and stuffed pink, silky cotton candy in her mouth until her stomach ached, and her jaws could no longer move for 15 minutes.

"Ahh, yes, why, earthlings always are pleased when they come here. Come meet Sunny." Amber gestured to a girl with blonde hair and freckles. *'She has a suntan,'* Bella guessed the girl had been spending lots of time on the Florida beaches.

"Hello. I'm Sunny and I come from Miami, Floria. I'm thirteen. My unicorn is Beatrice." She had a dainty voice tone. She gestured toward a unicorn with a baby blue colored mane and glasses. Amber had an amber colored mane.

"Hi." The unicorn introduced herself in a low voice. "I am Beatrice and I live near Genius Avenue, also where Sunny lives," she said in an even lower, solemn voice. Bella had to crane her neck to hear her.

"Yeah, hi. I'm Bella, this is Amber. Nice knowin' ya, bye!!" Bella said, quickly. She obviously wanted to get this over with.

"No! I mean, um, Bella, I think we should get to know each other a little more," Sunny requested.

"You have a really soft voice, so I can't hear you," Bella told her.

"Okay! I want to know more about you! Bella! Can you hear me?!" Sunny yelled.

"That's more like it. Okay, sure," Bella agreed, not too enthusiastically. "Do you want to race unicorns?" she asked.

"Do I?!" Sunny replied, and hopped onto her horse.

"Three...two...one!" Bella counted, and the two girls took off on their pair of beasts.

"Wow! You're fun, Bella!" Sunny said. Bella didn't mind her low voice now.

"Thanks," Bella said, blushing. She started thinking about her life and how much better off it was than others. But reader, oh, she was luckier than Riley would've ever been. Reader, she was thankful. But maybe on the other hand, she thought about the vampires. How the vampires tried to kill her and her friends. She could think about that.

"So, tell me about your life, Bella!" Sunny yell-said, curiously. "It must've been a pretty fun one!"

Bella chuckled.

They dismounted their horses.

"Well, actually..." she started, "kind of the opposite. It was really scary, pretty much! You see, I have this older sister, Stephanie." She paused, thinking about Steph. Where was Steph? Although she knew the answer. In Nova Scotia,

Canada. "Well, one time, she and I were forced to go to the mall by our parents, weirdly. Our mom and dad *never* sent us to a mall! But, we went, since, well, you know. It's *the mall*. Anyways, I got these cute butterfly hair clips, we got some lunch, fun! But when we got back, our mom and dad started arguing like crazy! Steph and I watched every little thing they did, and heard every little thing they said.—"

Sunny cut her off. "But isn't that eavesdropping?" she asked, worriedly.

"Nah. At least I don't think so," Bella told her.

"Okay, so back to the story, we were quite astonished by something my mother had said. She said... She said that she wanted a divorce. I was really upset by this news, but that was that. My dad moved to Canada, and I lived with my mom, before she died. After the divorce, I caught Steph watching something really inappropriate—Mom doesn't allow it—even though it is against the rule. I asked her politely—yes. Anyway, it's been very weird and scary from there. You see, my bestie, Riley Peterson, her parents had died because vampires killed them. We needed to fight them off with Pegasus, (or Pegsy for short), and Amber, and so that's why I'm here. To be safe. I also learned this." Bella shot out ice from her hand. "I have ice powers."

She focused her attention on the ice and sculpted a masterpiece.

A unicorn.

"WOW!" Sunny gushed.

"Yeah. Riley learned to do the same thing, but with fire—and lava!"

"Amazing!" Sunny shouted. "Could I do it?"

"I think you have to do something brave and something in a battle." Bella thought for a moment.

"Oh. Battles never ever happen here, in the Unicorn World," Sunny said, gazing at the ground.

"Is there a queen or king?" Bella's eyes were sparkling.

Sunny mounted Beatrice.

"Sure! Follow me!"

Bella mounted Amber. And they galloped off, silhouettes, in the violet horizon, the sky sprinkled with streaks of light pink and midnight blue. Bella had one thing to do. Sunny and Riley were coming too.

She had to find Stephanie, her sister.

'Hang in there, Steph. I'm coming to rescue you.'

ABOUT THE AUTHORS

SHRUTEE TAKALE lives in New Jersey with her awesome family, having fun and doing lots of writing, drawing and painting.

Shrutee loves animals, and loves helping nature. Shrutee co-founded SWANS. SWANS stands for Saving WIldlife And Nature Society. It's an awesome organization, which helps nature and animals, and that's just Shrutee's type of thing. She did a lemonade stand not too long ago with Sabine and a few of her other awesome friends, and donated the money to St. Huberts, the animal shelter nearby. She did the same thing two years before. She also saved a baby bird named Chirpy, who really needed help, and water.

Shrutee has won many prestigious awards in Visual Arts. She received the Award of Excellence/First Place in the state of New Jersey in the PTA Reflections Competition. She got these awards while in first grade and again in fourth grade.

Her hobbies are: Reading, drawing, writing, and many other things. At present, she is also writing the books *Shadow* and *Pet Squad*.

SABINE ERBRECHT is a 10-year-old girl, living with her weird and fun family and her dog, Avon, and cat, Meipy. She is writing the following three books and more: *Sloane, The Girl Wolf* and *One Out Of Three*. She grew up wanting to be a writer like J.K. Rowling and now she is. Kinda. Her hobbies are writing, reading, and traveling. Sabine is a proud and happy member of an awesome society (Work In Progress) called the SWANS. (Saving Wildlife And Nature Society). Her job is being in charge of helping animal shelters, helping get food for the shelter, and making sure stray animals come there for good homes. SWANS helps with climate change, global warming and saving trees and saving stray animals. What?! She and the club love animals!

Sabine is living in New Jersey, U.S.

Acknowledgements

I'D LIKE TO THANK my best friend/editor, Abigail Kim, and our wonderfully awesome editor, (and my aunt) Aunt Jacquie. Also, I'd like to thank my parents, John Erbrecht and Juliana Tozzi, of course, and most importantly, John, (Sonny) my fantastically awesome little brother. To all my family and friends. You are all great people. Thank you for your support. I'd also like to thank my teachers. I'd like to thank all the members of the SWANS, too. (And especially Shrutee, she the 3rd member and so great I wanna cry woop-woop!) Thanks to my dog, Avon, and cat, Miepy.

And again, I would love to thank Shrutee. I really couldn't have done it without you. Well, *we.* I love you as a bestie. Duh! I love you all! Like,

amilliontrillionfillionsomuchican'tcount!!!!!!!!!!

Thank you all so much.

S.E.

I WOULD LIKE TO THANK all the people who supported me and helped me in writing this book. My dad, my mom, my family. Sabine's Aunt Jacquie, the very awesome and wonderful editor, who is very wise. My aunt, my grandpa, and a gazillion others. Aaaand of course, Sabine. HOW WOULD WE HAVE DONE THIS BOOK WITHOUT EACH OTHER?! TELL ME! I love her very much. To the next universe. And beyond.

I'd like to thank my friend Sabine <Put a DUH!> I'd like to thank my teachers because, without them, I wouldn't have even been writing this book! I'd like to thank all SWANS members, future and present.

Thanks a
gazzilliongabajillionextrahugetimesithastoreachtotheotheru
niverse times!

ST.

PS. Riley has something to say.

"HI GUYS!!! I wrote a poem about my dad."

Ode To Dad (By Riley Peterson)

My father. Where will I start?
From the sleek brown hair to his dangerous driving.

The way his glorious dimples shone on his smile which made everybody's day a bit brighter, which caused a young girl to have twice as much energy as the full amount of energy an average girl should have.

The torture, unfortunately, was the goofiness to the side of his dimply smirk or grin.

The uncomfort it caused to some, and the joy it brought to many.

The way he could stand up for himself but in a very calm way was one of the very many quirks that made his way of living a bit more of his style.

His athletic form was a small advantage for his evening jogging.

The way he would people-watch as if he *wasn't* introverted, which he knew he was.

The way he would sheepishly give a person something and ask absolutely nothing in return showed it clearly.

Waking up in the morning, seeing his early-bird face with his casual black turtleneck and light-colored jean jacket with his beige khaki dress pants was the normal dress code of his.

His freshly shaved extended goatee and his slicked hair was a huge part of the majority of the outstanding outfit he would choose.

And the faces he would make, the goofy smile and personality, not to mention the cachinination and passion of his sophisticated chuckle or chortle would make any person beam from forty miles away.

As you helped raise and take care of me in such a charismatic and nurturing way.

I would give anything to have that back.

But I know that I don't need to have it back.

Not anymore.

Made in United States
North Haven, CT
25 July 2022

21824119R00122